Client Name: *Erica Black*

- Sneaking around in Church
- Birthcontrol switch
  Pregnancy Scare???

- Who gave who chlamydia?
- Turn up or Transfer?

I'm naive sexual
and newly educated

Inspired by some true events

Ciera Donielle

Freshman

gatekeeper press

Columbus, Ohio

Insane: Freshman

Published by Gatekeeper Press
2167 Stringtown Rd, Suite 109
Columbus, OH 43123-2989
www.GatekeeperPress.com

The cover design and editorial work for this book are entirely the product of the author. Gatekeeper Press did not participate in and is not responsible for any aspect of these elements.

ISBN (paperback): 9781662900433
eISBN: 9781662900440

Library of Congress Control Number: 2020938203

Contents

Acknowledgments

Writing this book has been a fantastic experience. God has blessed me with a gift that I can share with you all. I wrote this book with my two little sisters Amiah and Moriah Humphrey, in mind. They will be going to college soon, and I wanted to share my stories, hoping that it will help them become sexually aware and avoid the problems I faced. I want to thank God for everything. I want to express my love and appreciation for my parents, Ronda and Dondi Humphrey, for always pushing me and holding me accountable. I want to thank my village (grandmas, grandpas, uncles, aunties, church family, etc.) for encouraging me and keeping me deep in your prayers. Thank you for your support and love:

Tronaea Outlaw
Alexis McClain
Johnnie Harris

Shanelle Williams
Ronise Devore
Ollie McDonald
Rosetta Humphrey
Rhonda Craig
Kendra Dukes
Shanise Gabriel
Gaynell Green
Makalah K
Samuel Okeadu
Jennifer Blake
Rodnisha Graham
Morshe D. Araujo-*Editor*
Mousam Banerjee IG: illus_station- *Cover Design and Illustration*
CA$H-NTERTAINMENT
Bobby James "RockBoBsteR" producer/composer

A special thanks to Miranda Queen, author of *You Are Not the Father,* for your mentorship. Thank you for paying it forward and guiding me through the book writing process. I will do the same.

*"Once upon a time not long ago, I was a hoe, and I'm
admitting it. I WON'T take it back cuz I did the shit"*
—*Mariahlynn*

Call it! Time of diagnosis: 2:24 p.m. on the 16th day
of August. My name is Erica, and if I don't get my ish
together, I see myself buried by the time I hit forty, due to
stress. I'm twenty-four years old, thinking about death. I
have been called a drama queen my entire life, and to the
world and my family, that may be the case, but to me, in my
head, my problems are a big deal. It feels like the world is
against me; I'm all alone, and no one could possibly understand what I am going through. I think this way because
my brain works differently than others. Up until this day,
I allowed others to make up what they think my problem
is, they blame it on me being a Gemini. Well, that may

better help explain my "unstableness," but that cannot be the only reason, and since I am a broke college grad with two degrees and nothing to show for it, I need help sorting out my mind. I can't afford a counselor, so I am going to use you. At the end of it all, I need you to tell me what you think is wrong, better yet, it may be easier just to tell me what is right.

You're probably confused about where this is going so, let me give you a briefing. Eighty percent of my problems concern men, better yet the boys that have entered my life. No shade, I call them boys because I just said I'm twenty-four and let's be honest, what really makes a man a man? The other twenty percent are my other issues, like acceptance, self-worth, and trying to find myself. I'm not shy when it comes to sharing. I mean, how can I be if I expect you to give me your honest opinion. I can't withhold evidence of my insanity. A quick fact, I watch TV a lot—medical shows, lawyers shows, marvels—shit, everything. So, I may compare my situations with those which I have seen on TV. Sometimes I live in a fantasy world, which probably explains all the failed situation-ships. So, let's dive in.

Welcome to Counseling

I opened my eyes in my pitch-black room, beating my alarm clock by one minute. That was a surprise. Usually, I hit snooze about two times, but today felt special. My alarm on my Galaxy S9 read, 3:47 a.m., along with the heading, "1 YEAR DOWN HOW LONG CAN YOU GO". I died laughing because it wasn't even my work alarm. It was a day I marked in my calendar nine months ago. You will never guess the lengths I went through to find out the exact date. Well, not really lengths. LOL. I told you they call me a drama queen. Earlier this year, I was confident I was celibate for a year. I thought the last time I had sex was right after my birthday, June 5, but something inside told me to confirm. So, I clicked the search button in my text messages and searched common words I would have texted Roderick, my Texas first. If you could see me, you would know I was rolling my eyes even thinking about him. He will be featured later in the session.

I told you, you are my counselor, and I am laying on your couch, and it's not that comfortable if you ask me.

I typed in the word "pussy." Yeah, I said it, pussy, and multiple messages from the same number popped up. I am quick to block and delete people, but I like to keep all my receipts. I went to the bottom of the thread and read up until I found the message with my thirsty ass saying, "I still smell your scent in my room. I had fun last night."

A few messages under that was me asking when Roderick was going to take me out on a date and saying for what seemed to be the hundredth time, "I'm not talking to you no more until you take me out."

I'm just gonna say he was a King, just not my King. The important message, you know, the one with evidence of my last known date to bust it open, read August 7, 2017. Using that evidence and my recollection about how that day went, I came up with 3:47 a.m. on August 7 of last year as the last time I had sex.

I made it a year without having sex. I say I did it to cleanse my body from the negative, toxic souls that entered and to train myself to not to give up the booty before I get a date and anything nice out of it. I wanted to challenge myself because ever since I lost my virginity one month before my seventeenth birthday, I haven't gone longer than three months without sex. Throughout this entire year of celibacy, I've been sending thirst traps to the same nighas I was trying to cleanse from and a couple of guys that I knew but never fucked.

One month ago, I got really horny; I mean extremely horny. I watched porn every day – not your everyday porn – the kind of 'shit I would never do' porn. I know I'm not alone ladies because some women on Lip Service experienced the same thing. I searched for double penetration, gang bang, and hella lesbian shit like clit rubbing and ass eating, and when my cooch started pinching itself or squeezing close, I knew I was satisfied for the night. I don't know why but if I masturbate and my cooch throbs, my body is done with being horny for the moment, but when I am fucking a big dick ass negro, and my cooch starts throbbing all I want is more.

So, a couple of weeks ago, I realized my year was approaching, and I cold-turkey stopped sending thirst traps to all the nighas that I promised to lose my new v-card to, and I started focusing on this one guy I knew from back home, his name is Miles.

This guy was so cute to me in high school, and the fact that he was interested in me seven years later, nine hundred miles away, should have thrown up a red flag, but it didn't. We haven't seen each other since he graduated from high school in 2011. Why would he be interested in me? I already had plans to go home to visit family, so why not just sit on his dick while I was there.

Inner me: I'll tell you why not because you are worth more. You know your pussy is like a popsicle on a scorching hot summer day, and if a nigha is too thirsty, it's all gone before it can even melt away.

Sorry about that. My inner self is so deep. What she was trying to say was my shit is good. It's so damn good that ninety percent of the guys that received some of the magical loving nutted within ninety seconds of entering me. Give him a second chance, you say. Okay, second chance— five minutes without nutting what a waste of fucking time.

Damn! One day, I will listen to my inner self because if I did, I wouldn't be in this fucked up state of mind. I think I am incapable of listening to her. I'm geeked over dude because he said the right things and gave me the attention I needed. Well, he did at first. Isn't that how it always starts. Damn, why the fuck (tf) am I catching the signs after the fact. I told you my brain works differently.

I told my mom about him, her best friend, and of course, my girls. I even told Jade about him, and we are still trying to rekindle our friendship. We had a fall out at the end of junior year in college.

SMH E, if you knew better, you would do better.

8 p.m. I thought about nothing other than smashing, losing my V-card. I returned home from the store and emptied my bags on the marble bar top, and my best friend, Blake, yelled out, "Damn bitch! What you do? Go buy yourself a sex kit."

I looked down at the counter to figure out what she was eyeballing and laying there were breath mint strips, Summer's Eve wipe packets, and some other things. Damn, I thought to myself she caught me. I could do nothing but laugh. Then she hit me with, "Make sure he at least takes you out on a date before you give him some."

I wasn't trying to hear that; I convinced myself that I was just going to fuck Miles—fuck him and leave the feelings in his bedroom. I was going to fly back home and not give this man a second thought afterward. I honestly believed that could have worked if he didn't do to me what I tried to do to him.

August 10, 2018

My plane landed at Cincinnati/Northern Kentucky International Airport. I powered on my phone, and the first notification I received was from Miles, "let me know when you land so I can pull up."

Miles is tall, with buff arms and rock abs. I guess I kinda have a type. I love me some buff-ass men. He has big, round brown eyes with a clean fade and a sexy ass beard. He gives me Lakeith Stanfield vibes, the guy who plays Darius on the show Atlanta. Anyways, I'm geeked because he always said things to make me smile like, you know nigha shit.

I hit him back up and told him I landed, and he could pick me up from my mom's. Big Sexy picked me up all late and shit.

Another sign. Got dammit, Erica.

I was always trying to give a mf the benefit of the doubt. So, I changed my clothes to this cute orange spaghetti strap crop top and my big booty jeans that were tight as fuck (af).

I get to his car, no I'm not the chirp chirp girl, but a bitch still had to open her own door. What was I expecting, you ask? Well, in my fantasy world, I would have wanted him to pull up to my house and knock on the door, being that you haven't seen the kid in seven years. He could have even gotten out the car to give me a proper hug, then open the door to let me in.

> *Inner Self: I was telling you this shit as you were walking to his car, and you didn't listen. You have to demand respect. MF can't read your mind. So now you mad?*

Well damn, bih. Tell me how you really feel. Better yet, don't. You have no filter.

I got in his car, and we stopped at the gas station. He asked me if I wanted anything. Yay him.

> *Inner Self: from the gas station, really you happy because he offered to get you something from the gas station.*

We started back driving and headed to his house. Yes, you heard right. No freakin date. Straight to his crib, we went. In my defense, I convinced myself that I was the only one on vacation and everyone else still had lives they had to live. He had to get up early for work.

> *Inner self: Fuck that. You told this negro you were coming into town two months ago if he wanted to spend time with you, he would have made the time to do it.*

We arrived at his apartment. I grabbed my bag and the snacks Miles got me, and when I reached to open the car door, I noticed a pink flower make up bag on the side of the seat. My first thought was, "this nigha gotta girlfriend."

Then I talked myself down; I tried to rationalize. I remembered he told me he was leaving his mom's place before he picked me up. "He has a teenage sister; maybe the bag could have been hers," I thought to myself.

I washed it out of my mind and followed him to his apartment building. Miles kept pestering me, flicking my face, and smacking my ass. I stopped walking, "still childish, I see," I teased.

He got behind me and pulled me towards him. I ground my ass across his dick, trying to sneak a feel. He leaned down and kissed my ear. I tilted my head, then he kissed me on my cheek and sucked on my neck. I blushed; I felt so wanted. He was warm, his lips were soft, and I just wanted to be in that moment forever. Miles turned me around, and then it happened, our first kiss. I didn't do the whole lean in and leg up fairytale thing, but I did get butterflies.

We finally walked into his apartment building. We walked up the stairs, he opened his door, and we walked in. His living room was empty, no furniture, no TV, nothing. The only thing in sight was clothes that were thrown here and there and baby toys. When we walked past the toys, Miles immediately told me his roommate had a kid and that all the stuff in the living room was his roommates. It was like he was reading my mind; he answered my questions before I could ask.

We walked into his man cave. He had a basic young guy room; no bedroom set just a bed on a frame, no headboard. He had a brown six drawer dresser with his watches, lotion, cologne, and weed stash on top. He had a short black reclining chair next to his bed, and of course, he had a TV mounted on the wall, with a shelf underneath for his game. I sat in the chair and put my bag on the ground next to me. I grabbed the cherry flavored Twister drink; Miles got me out the bag and took a sip. My mouth was beginning to feel dry. Miles grabbed the weed from his dresser and sat on the bed. He tossed me the game controller and said, "find us a movie."

Miles grabbed a tray from underneath his bed so he could roll-up. After pretending I knew how to work his game system, I finally asked him if he could go to Netflix or Hulu. I could not find it, and he was just going to watch me struggle until I asked for help. I turned to *Bad Boy II*, and Miles sparked up. We talked for a bit, finished the blunt, then he made me join him on the bed. He kissed me passionately, sucking and biting on my bottom lip, you know the works. Then it happened.

Round one: He told me to take off the tight ass jeans I had on. You know, the ones I wore because I thought we were going on a date. I took them off and straddled him. He had these moments when he just stared at me. Now that I think about it, a few guys had those moments when they looked at me; call me crazy, insecure, or whatever, but that shit freaked me out. I'm not sure if I don't feel beautiful enough to be stared at, but we will come back to that later. I'm sure it has to do with my younger years. As he looked at me, he noticed the tattoos I had, and he was awestruck.

"I can't believe you are here in the flesh," Miles said to me, "right next to me. You so cold." He pulled me down to kiss him.

The mysterious voice in my head: Boy, how long you been liking me for real? Or is this what you say to get the panties off. TBH, spare me the mushy mushy, cuz I already had in my head we were going to fuck.

We kissed, and he loomed over me. "Take this off," he said, referring to my shirt. I'm always complicated, so of course, I said, "you want it off, take it off."

Once my shirt was gone, his tongue went to work. He kissed my lips, then used the tip of his tongue to lick my nipples. He came back up for a brief kiss to my lips then kissed all the way down to my stomach. He pecked the top of my freshly waxed cooch, and I took a deep breath because I just prayed this wouldn't be another situation when I brought the guy head back up. I wasn't a fan of head, and before I could even think of the second reason, I took another deep breath, and he went in—sucking and munching on my clit, causing me to jerk in a way I never have before with oral pleasure.

Oh shit, he did it; he broke the curse. He went in and made love to my pussy with his mouth; his tongue felt like the one shower setting you use to have the water beam down to massage your clit. I mean, seriously now, I'm thinking about it. I may be in love with his tongue. He pulled his fingers in and out of me while he sucked the soul out of Lady, and then I came.

*Lady is what I named my vagina. I deal with
three people, me, Shayla and Lady*

To be honest, I think I came a couple of times in his mouth. He sat up in front of me, lowered his shorts, and the mystery was over. I saw his dick for the first time. Was I impressed? I mean, his dick was skinny and about six or seven inches, the perfect size to lose my new-found virginity. It was my turn to do my most favorite thing, and as soon as my mouth touched his chocolate delight, I went blank. My mouth dried up, and I couldn't stop thinking about what needed to be done next. I had to teach myself how to give head again. I'm sure he wasn't aware of my trials and tribulations because he was surely fucking my mouth, but I know for sure that was probably the worst head I have ever given. This was me, "Okay, lick the head, suck on it; go all the way down."

Choke choke choke—eyes water.

Then I was like, "Move your hands up and down up and down, suck his balls. Oh, damn, he hairy af! Focus E, focus. Back to the dick, lick his shave, twirl your tongue around the head."

My mouth was so dry, it created this thick ass saliva, the kind you just want to spit out, but shit, I had no saliva to spare. Miles got up to get the condom. While he opened it, I put his dick back in my mouth and continued to suck until he put it on. He turned me around, bent me over, and slowly put his man's inside. Miles was so gentle with Lady, like she was his baby. He put his entire dick inside of me and gave me one big pump, and I nearly jumped out my skin.

My alter ego Shayla was like, "Bitch, I know it's been a minute, but you act like you can't take the dick. Don't make me come out."

He noticed that it was uncomfortable for me and turned me over to do missionary, the position he should have started with from the beginning. Don't get me wrong, I'm a backshot shawty, but in my Nicki's voice, you gotta prep me for shit like that.

To say the least, round one was awkward; we couldn't find our rhythm, and he came faster than a commercial break on a good ass lifetime movie. Miles got up and left the room. He came back moments later with a wet towel and two mini bottles of water. I grabbed the towel and water. I took the water to the head, then wiped myself off with the towel. We laid down, sitting in our thoughts.

Inner voice: "Got dammit E, you wasted yet again another fuck."

Miles wasn't going down like that. He had to prove he could last longer than five minutes. I like it when nighas challenge my pussy because she makes grown-ass men tap out, but I like it even more, when they win the challenge. Miles pulled out his dick, and Shayla said, *"Fuck this bitch; I'm going in."*

Shayla took control of my body, leaving poor 'ol Erica playing a game of Temple Run in la-la land. I got on the side of him and put the tip of my tongue on the head of his dick then, tooted my chocolate ass up. He smacked my ass, and I made his dick disappear. It was like riding a bike. I guess

Miles had to break me in a little bit before Shayla came out. Miles started to fuck my mouth. After making myself gag about four or five times, I pinched my lips around his dick and came up slowly. I licked down his shaft and started sucking his balls. Miles turned his freak on, gently grabbing my leg, placing my pussy right on top of his face. I don't know what it is about men, but they love to tease. He gave my lady parts delicate sweet kisses that quickly turned into licks. I stopped mid suck—my face and hands, covered in saliva—because I could no longer focus. By this time, I regained control of my body and began to challenge Miles as well. Let's just say I got my championship belt back for being the Queen of back shots, and he for sure had the time of his life.

Congratu-fuckin-lations Miles, you took my virginity. Well, my new virginity.

We fell asleep and woke up about two hours later; then it turned back awkward. Not because we just fucked but because I felt like I had just relapsed.

Relapse, you may ask. Well, to fully understand what I mean, we got to start from the beginning.

Chapter 2

Born a Freak

I, Erica Danielle Black, was born in Cleveland, VA.

Listening to stories from my family, I was basically a freak all my life.

I was quite the kid. I ran around the house when I was five years old butt-ass naked screaming, "Bucky naked." Swinging the clothes that were once on my body around my head.

I called myself having a boyfriend when I was seven, and he lived next door. I managed to convince my big cousin to write this nasty, freaky love letter to him. Summer was two years older than me, so she knew how to spell more words than I did, and she knew how to write in cursive. Fancy, right?

The letter read something like this:

Dear Boyfriend

I love you; I want to kiss you a lot. I want to freak you on the ceiling fan. I want to kiss you on the swing tomorrow when we play.

Luv E

People usually skip over Erica and go straight for E.

I made Summer rewrite the letter, making it neater, and she tossed the draft in the trash. Why out of all the days to go digging in the trash, my Uncle Jayce, Summer's dad, looked in the fucking trash. Later, we found out he saw us, let him say it "looking sneaky," by the garbage can so he went to investigate.

Instead of busting our asses as soon as he found out, he decided to set us up. He let me get almost lip to lip with the little boy then scared the shit out of us with a belt. Yeah, he whooped my boyfriend's ass too. I got another ass whooping, with Summer, when she came back in from playing. He said I got one whooping for thinking of a letter that was not ladylike and another one for attempting to follow through on it. Summer got her ass whooped for assisting me in such freak, nasty behavior.

2002

I experienced head before I even knew what it was.

I slept with my dog and let him lick my vagina.

2003

My introduction to porn.

I walked in on with my older cousin Farris watching porn and jacking off. He didn't know I came into the room; I was being sneaky.

Another day, Farris was supposed to be watching me, but instead, he took me to the basement and stuck me in front of the TV. I got hungry, so I came upstairs. I heard voices in his room on the second floor. I called his name on the stairs remembering I wasn't allowed on the second floor without permission. Farris came out of his room, butt ass naked. He looked like he just busted a nut, all sweaty, and his dick was flimsy as ever. He didn't even try to hide it.

2004-2005

Summer and I found my mom's stash of porn DVD's.

I used my first condom

My mom was gone to work for a few hours, so I got to stay home by myself. I went into her nightstand and grabbed a sliver wrapped condom and one of the DVDs from her stash. I went into my room, put the DVD in my portable DVD player, and put the condom on this small, skinny, red, wooden bat my mom got from a baseball game. I slid my new toy inside me and experienced a lot of pleasure. I was so curious.

I can't believe I have been holding all of this in for, for shit, since it happened. To be honest, this isn't even most of the beginning. Do you need a break? I would say I know you're charging me by the hour, but you're not. I do, however, appreciate you hearing me out.

No break, okay? Well, can you at least offer me a glass of water? I've been talking so much, my mouth dried out. Okay, okay, I'm reaching back to it.

I was born a chocolate girl with a head full of hair— my parents' perfect little angel. I was raised by a single mother in her twenties, and if you ask me, she did a fantastic job. My parents' divorced a little after I was born, so I never had a chance to see a "real" relationship. My mother dated but nothing serious, and I am sure my father dated, but I never met his women. The things I'm going to share with you, my parents don't even know. So, thank God for patient-doctor confidentiality.

I thought I was the most beautiful girl until I started going to school, and the kids there quickly pointed out my flaws. I was called everything: a horse, monkey, blacker than black, charcoal. The kids at my school really broke me down. I honestly felt like I was hideous. The boys I had a crush on never made fun of me to my face, but they were always the first to laugh. I hated everything about me; my skin complexion, the big black mole covered by my big nose. Imagine that, a child, hating herself for something she had ultimately no control over.

My mom always called me beautiful; she was supposed to. The village that helped raise me always tried to make me feel good enough, but I just didn't. Children are cruel sometimes, and my village did not have to sit there and take those capping sessions. It was not until my second-grade year when my teacher, Ms. Lyfe, sat me down after class and told me how beautiful I was. This talk felt different from the talks with my mom because Ms. Lyfe did not have to tell me I was beautiful and how to try to love my mole at least. Take the time to get to know it, so that I can accept it.

I tried everything to get rid of all my flaws. Ms. Lyfe witnessed me trying to cut off my mole with a pair of safety scissors, and that's when I was forced to put an end to my DIY plastic surgery madness. Right after that, I started getting attention from boys, maybe because I let them touch my butt. I forgot all about my mole next to my nose, but I could not change or feel good about my skin complexion.

In my elementary school days, if it was light, then it was right. No shade, but not every light skin girl is cute and thank God for our chocolate sisters being more published now – #IssaRae #RyanDestiny #LupitaNyong'o #ReginaeCarter; I can't forget the legends #OprahWinfrey #NoamiCampbell and so many more. So, believe me when I say there are some beautiful chocolate women. Beautiful women come in all shades.

I started off young doing things to get attention from boys, anything really to make them like me. I started using my body at an early age, letting my crushes of the quarter smack my ass in the hallway. Don't get me wrong. My dad was present; he just didn't live with me. He and my mom split custody. I really didn't know a thing about him, and he really didn't know me. I was never really taught the right way a man is supposed to treat you. I knew my father loved me with his entire heart; I mean, I was his first baby girl, but I never felt comfortable enough to talk to him about it. I wanted to be a perfect angel to him. So how was I supposed to learn the right and wrong ways to get a boy to like you? I had to learn from experience. Which explains the rest of what I am about to tell you.

Let me start off by saying this is a NO JUDGEMENT ZONE. Let him who has not sinned cast the first stone… I'll wait. NOT.

Good Girl Gone Bad

Paul: First Boyfriend

I was in the eleventh grade, in love with my church crush, until I met Paul—my first. I lost my virginity at sixteen, one month before my seventeenth birthday. I'm not going to lie; I was ready for it. So, does that mean Paul was just lucky, or did I have real feelings for him? To be honest, I convinced myself it was real feelings. Now that I am twenty-four, he was lucky. I lost my virginity to him a month after we dated and a month after getting the keys to my first car. Parents, not to ruin it for your kids, but this opened up the doors to my fuck-dom. Oops, I mean freedom.

My first time was nothing too special; we were watching Friday. Wait, before I tell you that, let me tell you what my fast ass did the night we started dating. I had been cruising the streets of Blue Woods, the same place I met

Paul, with my badass friend Justice. At the time, Justice was talking to Paul's cousin Jacob. So, of course, I was the tag-along friend. I called myself that because I was super scary as a kid, which I should have been. Shit, my mother was crazy. She didn't have to prove to me she was crazy. I felt it when she spoke. So, I, for sure, showed my mom respect. Well, up until that night.

After tagging along with Justice, Paul and I became a little acquainted with each other. It was almost time to leave, but I had to use the bathroom, so Justice and I ended up in Paul's house. Let's be clear, Paul's mama house. After using the bathroom, I walked out, and my phone chirped. It's a text from Justice. "Girl, so what you gone do because I am not about to sit in this car and hear what you shoulda coulda woulda done?"

I don't know if I read that text message aloud because Paul said, "Come here real quick. I got something I want to show you in my room."

Oh shit! My heart started pounding. The most I had done was get fingered in the Rec Center at my Catholic high school by a senior football player during my freshman year. Oh yeah, and I jacked off my church crush in the church hallway.

Hey, didn't I say this was a no-judgment zone?

I walked into Paul's pitch-black room. He shut the door then started kissing me. I'm like okay "straight to it," I thought to myself. He picked me up, threw me on the bed, and started to lick me through my panties. I thought

I was a professional fucker because I just knew what I was doing. Ha, so I thought. He pulled my panties to the side, then eventually off, and he went to town. *Sidebar: when I say he went to town, that does not mean I enjoyed it. I still have not gotten my socks knocked off due to head. Well, not until Miles got a taste.* Paul had absolutely no idea what he was doing. I thought he would be kind of experienced because he had kids. He licked nothing but the vagina. He stuck his tongue in and out like it was a substitution for his dick. His tongue made it to my clit a few times when he licked Lady like a kitten. Paul made one big ole mess. It instantly gave me flashbacks to when I had my first kiss at twelve.

Mylon from across the street. My real first boyfriend, he lasted about two months. My cousin Summer set the entire thing up. My mom left the house, and Summer and her friend went outside and invited Mylon over; I had no idea. Summer led him upstairs to my room, pushed him in, and shut the door. We heard Summer and her friend on the outside of the door yelling, "kiss, kiss, kiss."

Mylon was a tall skinny fourteen-year-old. He had scars on his face like he been scratched up by cats all his life, and his front teeth overlapped each other. The night before the setup, Mylon's brother accidentally elbowed him in his face and chipped his tooth.

Summer and her friend would not let up. They kept opening the door to see if we had done it yet and refused to let us out if we hadn't kissed. All I could think about was my mom pulling up and beating my ass. I felt like that was going to be a wooden paddle beating; she saved her paddle for the good shit. I took a deep breath and said, "fuck it."

I leaned in to kiss him. It started off as a peck, but then baby boy started to feel himself, he started sticking his tongue in my mouth. I had no idea what to do; I was so in my thoughts. Seconds after we started tongue kissing, I felt saliva sliding down my chin to my neck. It was so disturbing. I hate saliva; the shit is nasty. I mean, I don't mind my own, but the thought of someone else's, no. I ended the kiss with a peck then pushed him away. Summer opened the door almost instantly after. She seen me wipe my neck and chin, laughed, then offered me a towel. One big messy ass mess just like Paul.

Paul's saliva was all down my ass cheeks and inner thighs. I assumed that was how it was supposed to be, so I tried my best to enjoy it. Of course, I felt like I was doing something, which I wasn't doing shit. My friends had been there done that, but they called me "fast." We walked out of his room, and that was that. Paul was my boyfriend, and I just got my pussy ate. Boss Shit, right? Not at all.

Shortly after, a month and three days, to be exact, I lost my virginity. As I said earlier, we were watching the movie Friday. It was nothing special, just a regular afternoon. I don't know why, but I was feeling super freaky. Maybe because the day before, I chilled with my church crush at his cousin's house, and let's just say it definitely got steamy but not too much before I had to remember I was in a relationship. Damn.

I was sitting next to Paul on the edge of the bed wearing a sundress, and he was shirtless with basketball shorts. I placed my hand on his dick gave it a light squeeze. Paul leaned back on the bed, and the sunbeams that peaked through his window gleamed on his chest. I put my hand down his shorts and pulled out his dick. It was soft and squishy until I cover it with my soft brown plump lips. I gave him delicate strokes with my tongue, witnessing him grow inside of my mouth. "Finally," I thought to myself, "I got to experience sucking dick."

I felt accomplished because Blake had already given head and told me I should try it. So, I did, and I was kinda awesome at it. He felt absolutely no teeth, and I heard him moan. I guess I should thank the white girls in porn for the lesson.

Don't act like you didn't watch porn when you were a teen. I got into all my mom's DVDs. I honestly think she introduced me to Mr. Marcus, and she doesn't even know it.

I gave him one last lick, put his dick in my mouth, then pressed my lips and my tongue against it and slowly came up. I wiped my mouth, and Paul got up, gave me a kiss, and pushed me down on the bed. He gave me some of his tongue magic then rubbed his dick back and forth across my pussy. Lady was so wet, and I just imagined what it would feel like to have him inside of me. I grabbed his dick and guided him in. To my surprise, it didn't even hurt. He just slid right in. Notice I didn't say he put on a condom. After all them damn Sex Ed talks, I let this mutha fucka fuck me raw. This is clearly not the only fuck up that occurs in my life, so buckle up; it's gonna be a fucked-up ride.

Why did we break up, you ask? Well, the fucker cheated on me multiple times with ugly girls. I'm not a hater; I always give girls their props if they are beautiful, but these bitches weren't. His disrespectful ass made me feel like I wasn't shit, and I had to deal with it. I accepted the apologies, and I hear your questions. No, his ass never took me out on a date. Well, once but I had to drive there. No, his black ass never bought me anything. Wait, yes, he did on Valentine's day when I drove him to the store. He went in to get me a Heath bar, an unsigned V-day card, and a small white bear that I later tossed in the backyard to my big Boxer for him to rip to shreds. Paul's fuck ups made it easy for me to slip back to this guy.

My Church Crush

Disclaimer: This next guy plays a significant role in my life, but he is very insignificant.

Dante was everything I thought I wanted in life. I liked him since I was eleven. He was the preacher's son and my first love. One of those loves where he was my everything, but he didn't even know I existed. I was utterly obsessed with this boy, his smile even with them braces, his smell even though his mama probably had to force him to wipe his ass and his chocolate skin. Dante probably didn't notice me until I turned thirteen. I was more developed and started to wear more flashy clothes.

The term Flashy for the sake of this sentence means revealing— revealing enough to seduce a 14-year-old boy, but not enough to get popped by grandma.

Then it happened. Dante kissed me in the hallway at church, where all my unchristian fast behavior started.

We were definitely some childish ass kids, though, because the kissing process took forever. My church was super big and super old. We had a big church for the adults upstairs and children's church in the basement. I was sitting in Children's Church, wearing this tube silk fluffy dress I got from DEB. Do you remember that store? Anyways, I got up to go to the restroom. In actuality, I was just bored, so I needed a distraction.

Kids, right?

On my way back downstairs to return to church, I stopped at the water fountain. Dante appeared much like how the other encounters began. He came behind me at the fountain and brushed his dick across my ass. It gave me the chills instantly. I knew it was him because I saw him walking out of Children's Church when I was coming down the stairs, that's why I stopped for water. I knew he was going to say something to me, but I didn't expect the preacher's son to be so bold. He pulled me out the sight of the children's church window near the creepy closet by the stairs. He played this little game where he said, "So, I hear you like me? I always thought you were cute." I'm geeked because this boy stood so close to me. So close, his little friend joined us, aroused "by my beauty," I assume.

Then Dante grabbed my hand and guided it down to touch his dick, and it was like my body knew what I was supposed to do because my cooch started to throb. He told me how beautiful my lips were and leaned in; his small soft lips touched mine. I'm sure he felt my heart pounding out of my chest as we kissed and ground against each other through our clothes. That happened so often, my favorite part about Sunday was seeing this boy.

We exchanged numbers, and this is when I think Crazy Erica evolved. Here's how our correspondences typically went. I'd text him, he'd respond, then we'd continue to text a little more. I started to get in my feelings then. All of a sudden, there was no response from him. Think that stopped me? No. Three text messages in a row. Still no response. I called my friend. "Hey girl, text this number and tell me if they text back."

Thirty seconds later, my friend said, "That number texted back, asking me who I am. Want me to respond?"

Fuck! This boy was ignoring me, but why?

I hope that's not judgment, I smell. I was
thirteen sheesh give me a break.

Looking back at it now, I needed to feel wanted. My heart was filled the most when Dante showed interest in me, so whenever he stopped paying attention to me, which was often, I felt the need to get it back. Even if it meant I was his second choice. Throughout high school, I was his second choice. Now don't get me wrong I had fun in high school, and I talked to other guys, as long as it was not on Sunday, that was Dante's day.

Dante was a popular guy. We didn't go to the same school, but our city isn't that big, so we knew the same people. He played sports, and every girl was on him. The older we got, the more our chemistry grew, so I thought. Looking back at it, the more I developed, the more Dante was interested. We started to see more of each other because our high schools were rivals. He went to Blue Woods Highschool. *See how that soon turned into a conflict of interest?* Dante played football, and I cheered. We both ran track, and every chance I got, I used it as an opportunity to make him want me.

We were competing at the same track meet one day, and Dante looked fine as ever. He was no longer wearing braces, and his teeth were perfect and white, totally complimenting his chocolate skin tone. I witnessed first-hand all the Blue Woods girls and a couple of girls from Journey High, an all-girl catholic school flock around this boy like he was a superstar or something. The girls on my team already knew he was off-limits; they were more into the Cape High boys, a black high school that breeds nothing but athletes. I didn't even try to get his attention. I just prepared for my race.

My uniform was a brown speed suit that practically looked painted on my body. It definitely complimented my ass. Dante might of had him a flock, but I had one of my own, two of them were Cape boys. I went up to the stands to grab water from my bag and speak to my mom, and my dad who surprised me. He flew into town to see me race. Dante's parents, Pastor Mike and First Lady Mia, noticed me standing next to my parents. They waved to me; I was trying to avoid them because Dante was over there with Stassi, his ex, I think. I'm not sure of her title, but I just knew she liked his ass.

Dante took that opportunity and walked over. He gave my mom a hug and thank God my dad went to the concession stand. He gave me a hug and asked me what race I was getting ready for. "The 200- meter dash," I responded

Right after I told him, they made the first call for my race. "Time to check-in," Dante said, walking down the bleachers with me.

We made it to the inner field. He volunteered to help me stretch. We shared a few laughs and love taps, but not too many before Stassi brought her ass over. By that time, Dante's relay team joined us. They all asked me about my race and congratulated me on dusting the girls in my heat for the 100 meter dash. Stassi inserted herself in every question they asked me. They made the last call for my race, and I got up to get in place. Dante stared me down. He watched me walk to my lane, lift my ass when the umpire yelled "set," and dust the girls in my heat. I barely showed him attention. He caught up with me at the finish line, and we walked toward the bathrooms, I gave him a peck, grabbed his dick then walked away. He was also wearing a speed suit. Even though I was still a virgin at the time, I knew how to get an erection out of any guy.

I guess my harmless talents weren't enough for him to make me his girlfriend. He had countless girlfriends, and I sat there like I wish it were me. Why couldn't it be me? Now I really had to face him. I wasn't going to be his church hoe anymore. I loved him, but he didn't ever choose me, only on Sundays. His best line for those thoughts was, "Erica, I love you. I'm sorry. I told every girlfriend that I've had that I'm always gonna choose you."

Yes. Yes. For two seconds, you can pass judgment because I fell for it.

Once I started driving and got my car, I really fell for the Okie Doke.

In between a few of Dante's girlfriend adventures, I stopped fucking with him. I was tired of sneaking off and pleasuring him.

So, some time had passed. I was eighteen, still dating Paul, so in love, until he cheated on me—broke my little heart. Because of me desperately wanting to feel wanted, I took him back. But this time, I wanted to play, so I did, and in doing so, I fell for Dante's trap again. We upgraded from Sunday Hallway Sessions to frolicking in my car, where we sat outside his parents' house whenever he felt like dealing with me. I noticed that he never invited me in. So, once I questioned him about that, I started asking him everything.

"Why haven't you made me your girl? Why you have everybody thinking it's me following you when it's you who won't leave me alone? Do you even really love me?"

This dude hits me with, "I don't want to make you my girl because I cheat on all of my girls with you. We about to go to college, and I don't want to risk what we have."

Yep, I fell for the bullshit. But not for long. Short story shorter, I let him hit it right before I went off to school. It was the wackest shit ever. In all that chemistry I thought we built—you know, in the hallway, my car outside his parents' house and oh yeah, through them long, one-way messages, the ones he stopped responding to—this human even fucked me selfish. The only foreplay he engaged in was kissing me and sucking on my neck. Does that even count as foreplay these days? Regardless, I was gushing wet; I was always wet around him. He was the love of my life. When he fucked me, I could tell his objective was to bust his nut and not to please me. I was a "fucking dummy," literally and figuratively.

Talk about bang bang bang, Ouch! Word on the street, well on his parents' street, I took his V-card. Y'all believe him? Nah, me either, but oh well. He was done, and Paul and I were hanging on by a thread, and I mean the thinnest thread, with my insecure ass. I went off to college and basically snipped that thread right in half within three weeks after meeting a guy named Tali.

Chapter 4

Welcome to Undergrad

Freshmen year, I arrived a couple of weeks early to campus for track practice. I swear that was the longest drive ever. My mom and grandma followed my little sister and me down to my new home, one state over. Jackson H University, one of two historically black colleges and universities (HBCU), in Kentucky. Since they were following me down, I drove the speed limit. I didn't want to give my mom any reason to reconsider her decision to allow me to bring my car down. One of her conditions was not getting any tickets. If I caused her insurance to increase, I was going to be cut off. As far as the insurance company knew, my car was in Cincinnati parked in my mom's driveway.

We left the city and headed to what appeared to be the country. The only scenery around were horses, cows, and cotton fields. I started to question if I was looking at the same fields my ancestors picked from. The drive took about two hours and fifteen minutes. My grandma grew tired of my slow driving and went around me. My heart finally slowed its pace. It felt like having the police follow behind you; then, they finally get over. I turned on No Lie by 2 Chainz, relaxed my shoulders, leaned back in my seat, and blasted my music from the new speakers my dad just installed when he visited me.

We arrived on campus and followed the signs to my dorm. As soon as I got out of the car to unload my things, all I saw were Fine Ass Black Men. I knew I was going to have a fun college experience. Lucky for me, my roommate never showed up. She was there as far as the school knew, but she really stayed with her boyfriend. On my first day of practice, I walked up to the stadium for a check-up and sickle cell test and met my knight in shining armor, let the eighteen-year-old me tell it. Tali was always this loud, goofy, cool guy with a hood side. Zaddish right?

Shut up, I was eighteen, and that was everything. Tali is about 5'10 and dark chocolate. He had mild acne on his face, and he had dreads. I could tell his muscles hadn't fully peaked, but he was nicely built. He also had something about him that I just needed to experience. It was like a vampire passing a human that smelled amazing but then saw that same human a week later after he'd been starving.

I was ready to pounce, but I played it cool at first.

I was with all these upper-class athletes, and I was fresh meat trying to stay out of the way. Then here comes James, a senior. God, he had a body for days, a body that made you want to rub him down in oil and pounce on him. He was built like Thor, tall, fresh prince cut, big brown eyes, and caramel complexion. He must have sniffed me out of the pack; he had a mission. I'm not sure if he placed a bet on me or what, but it was too good to be true. This man wanted me. I could tell by his eyes. Think I'm crazy? You will soon understand I was born with a gift, sometimes I may come across as gifted, but I was born with a gift. I know when people—men and women—are interested in me. My reasonings may be a little unorthodox, causing my friends to question my sanity, but at the end of the day, when I know, I know. A gift, right?

The next day or so, I saw James at the bookstore where I started working the day I quit the track team. Yeah, I was tired of running. I wanted to enjoy myself, and shit, I was just too damn lazy. The bookstore was inside the student center on the second floor across from the student food lounge and cafeteria, and it had absolutely no privacy. It had big glass windows, and my manager made sure we Windexed and dusted all the time. Toward the back of the store was a little more privacy because all the fixtures blocked the view. James saw me through them large ass windows. He came in and immediately started flirting, asking me how old I was, if I was single, and then he called me a quitter. He had my attention until Tali walked past those same big ass bookstore windows. I pretended to work as I admired the view. I tuned out of whatever it was James was talking about and gazed at Tali. James eventually got the hint at least for the day.

Freshmen Week

Freshmen week is the week before the first day of classes. A week from the first day of classes, and as most HBCU alumni know, was one of the livest weeks ever. Not only for the freshmen but for everyone. The yard was packed. I was in the bookstore working, missing my first college event. I took my fifteen, which turned into a thirty-minute break. I just combined my two fifteen-minute breaks. You could hear the band playing from inside the student center. All the Greeks were out except the reds; they were suspended that year. The JH Scarlets danced their butts off to the school's anthem. Flyers went out for the freshmen bash at Emma's; believe me; everybody was going. The upperclassmen were going because shit, it was a bar, and they wanted to scope out the fresh meat.

Emma's was the spot for all the major parties at school—ladies two-for-five dollars vodka shots at the door. You remember that New Amsterdam? College was life. My homegirls and I walked into the bar, and you could tell we were freshmen. We were there hella early, shit, the lights were on, and the locals were still there. Lucky for me, Tali and his crew didn't get the memo either. He was just sitting there, vibing to the music in his own zone. The party got bigger and bigger, so you know girls' leave outs were sweating out, but everybody was lit. In between swag surfin', beefing it up to Do it by Mykko Montana, and ignoring Paul's repeated phone calls, I managed to down a few drinks and really get in my zone.

The DJ started the slow jams. I started moving and winding my hips to the beat, grabbed a chair because I was really feeling the music, and guess what? Tali grabbed me.

Phones went up, flashes were bright, but at that time, at that moment, it was just him and me. He picked me up, bent me over the chair, put me on his shoulders as I rode his face, we had the party watching us. I knew right then, like a vampire, I had to attack. That dance led me to the rest of the decisions I made at Jackson H University. Well, the sexual ones, at least. I later told my girls Jade and Kristy that I was gonna fuck the shit outta him. The song ended, and Tali gently put me down. Jade yelled, "Aye, dread head! What's yo name?"

He answered, "Tali (taw-lee) from Jamaica," then walked away

I came to my senses and begged my friends not to tag me in their footage. I didn't want them to post me at all dancing with Tali. More importantly, I didn't want Paul to see it. I got lucky that time. A few days after the party, while restocking the bookshelves, I plotted a way to get in

Tali's pants. Nothing I ever thought of was even close to how it went down. After work, Jade and I cruised around campus and passed Ivan Hall, where Tali and Cory, Jade's new boy, stayed. Cory was outside just in time to hop in my car to head to the store, then BOOM. Tali appeared. Jade's rachet ass told me to roll down my window, reached across me, and yelled, "Tali! What you about to do?"

Tali said, "Shit," then walked toward my car by the driver's side window.

"Wanna come to Walmart with us," Jade asked?

Tali agreed. I got out of my car to push down my seat so he could get in. This was the start of something great, so, I thought. I'm in this fantasy box in my head, thinking yep he's gonna be one of my baes.

He was great at Walmart, pushing the cart and everything. We talked, and I felt like it was a vibe. I felt so comfortable around him. We even went to the video game aisle and raced each other in the car racing game. We left the store and headed back to campus. Jade and Corey sat in the backseat, and Tali and I continued to get to know each other. I parked in my dorms parking lot; we got out and headed towards the yard. I left the things I purchased in my car. Tali and I sat in front of the student center under the flag poles facing the yard. Jade and Corey went off somewhere. Tali told me about his life.

When he was in middle school, he had been adopted by his uncle and aunt after his brother, Boogie, died from gang violence. Tali's uncle trapped, and his auntie was a pimp. I couldn't ask him what happened to his parents because I felt like if he wanted me to know, he would have mentioned it. There I was shocked that he told me all of this personal information. He continued to say how his uncle was mad at him because he wasn't on the streets working for him but decided to go to college. He changed the subject and asked me what's up. "Well, at the party, you picked me up and was dancing, and I wanted to fuck the shit out of you ever since," I replied.

In the midst of me telling him that, my friend Kristy walked up. Tali instantly grabbed his phone and called D, one of his friends from his dorm, to entertain Kristy. I guess D was supposed to be Captain Save-a-Hoe. Tali ain't shit. He used D to get Kristy away so he could fuck. Once D came up to the yard, he noticed the setup and figured he might as well get some pussy too. Kristy was down because she just turned eighteen and wanted some birthday sex. Kristy and I left Jade to play with Corey, and we followed the hornballs to their dorm.

We all walked down the lightly lit walkway towards Ivan Hall. The yard was quite no one was out except for us. Tali came up with this master plan to "sneak" us in. At HBCU's, the dorms are "strict." Well, they try to be. Ivan Hall was co-ed, but the floors were separated by gender. Visitors must be signed-in at the front desk and are only allowed during visiting hours. The first three weeks of semester Jackson H issued a campus wide "No Visitation" policy. A Bitch was taking risk for the dick.

Tali and D went to their room to grab our disguises. Kristy and I sat on the stairs in front of their dorm, so we wouldn't look like we didn't belong. Bambi and her babies walked passed us and headed toward the same walkway we left. "I wonder if they are in night school," Kristy joked.

"Shit, they might be," I said and laughed.

Tali came down with two hoodies. He said, "Here's D's key card. Put these hoodies on, walk up the steps, don't look suspicious, and don't look at the cameras." Kristy and I did just that, sneaking like we were still in high school.

Kristy and I walked up four flights of stairs, finally reaching their floor. I used the key card and tried to open up the door to get on their floor. I waved the key across the sensor again for the second time, and the light flashed red, making a short ringing noise like it was telling me access denied. Kristy grabbed the key from me and tried. Red light again, "damn this nigha card broke?" I asked.

We saw the dorm security coming up the stairs through the reflection on the stairway windows. Kristy tried the card again, finally green light. We opened the door and sighed in relief. I looked down the long ass hallway with white floors, looking like the psyche ward floors. My bougie dorms had carpet flooring and gave you hotel vibes, not I'm in the crazy house vibes, all sharing one stinky ass bathroom. Judgmental much? Sorry, I can't help it. Why am I talking all this shit? I stayed visiting Ivan Hall; all my friends lived there.

As we stared down the hall, Tali opened his room door and guided us in. We walked in, then noticed this man-made wall of dressers and two computer desks. Only one side of the room looked lived in, and that was the side Tali guided me to. The other side had no sheets on the bed, no decorations on the wall, and nothing on the shelves. It was apparent this was Tali's room, and D was not his roommate. So, looking back, this was a super set up, but let me continue. I went on Tali's side and sat on the bed. Tali turned off the lights and wasted no time. He kissed and licked me on my neck until our kisses were interrupted by Kristy's giggles.

"Is this nigha tickling her?" Tali whispered. I shrugged and offered a giggle of my own before Tali laid me down and slid my panties off. He leaned over to grab a condom.

Good job, E!

I felt him break through my walls like I was a virgin. It had been a couple of weeks since I had sex, so I was practically a virgin. He picked me up, bent me over, and fucked me like I never been fucked. This was sex. He was bigger than Paul, more ambitious than Paul, and most importantly, he was here, unlike Paul. I got what I wanted; I always get what I want. Well, I at least fuck who I want. I mean it; you'll see. Round one was over, he took off the condom, wiped off, and I laid on his chest. I asked, "How was it?"

Tali released a deep breath, smacked my ass, and said, "Good shit, Ms. Wet Wet." He rubbed my clit and noticed I was wetter than ever. He pulled me on top of him. His dick was standing at full attention, reminding me of a bob-blehead because it was moving back and forth, not reaching its target. Still, I straddled Tali, reached behind me, grabbed his dick, and rode him until his toes curled. This time no condom.

I was in love, child. This man fucked me good, and he fucked me raw. We about to be together.

Okay, I was eighteen and totally inexperienced.

Chapter 6

Mixed Liquor

I was always at Tali's dorm, but not exactly for him, I had friends that lived there, and okay, I was plotting to run into him. When Tali hit me up, I would always respond in my feelings, and he would stop texting. I was never the double texter, but I'm sure I double texted him a time or two. One-night, Jade and I took a trip to the liquor store with Corey, D, and a new guy Emmanuel. This ride was crazy. None of us was twenty-one, but D took us through the drive-thru in his decked-out 2016 dark grey, Hummer. Fancy, huh? My mom always said she wanted a Hummer, and I got to ride in one. "Kristy better play her cards right. D was riding nice," I thought to myself.

He pulled up to the drive-thru to order. I felt like I was presidential pulling up, his windows were tinted so dark that the white man at the window only saw his reflection. "What yal sipping on tonight?" D asked as he rolled his window down.

Jade and I split a fifth of Peach Cîroc, D got a bottle of E&J, and I'm almost certain Corey was drinking lean. I was too scared to try the lean, but Jade was down for whatever. *Okay, I lied. I did take a sip, but just enough to taste.* On our short trip back to campus, Jade was sipping Corey's drink, and I was staring at my phone, hoping Tali had hit me back up. He didn't.

Somehow the entire car knew what went down in the room with D and Tali and insisted that we talk about it. I had to take me a shot. D didn't participate much in the conversation because he was embarrassed; he'd "lowered" his standards and had sex with Kristy. She wasn't the prettiest, but beauty is in the eye of the beholder. I felt like all she needed was a makeover, just so it would spark more confidence. I could tell that she was insecure and doing things for attention. Her personality was a bit much; she liked to get attention. She was the type of a girl to get loud and extra if a guy she's attracted to is near her. Cory, Emmanuel, and Jade clowned D asking how he could fuck her then they asked if he would do it again. We pulled back on campus and headed toward their dorm.

We parked in the student parking lot in front of Ivan Hall with music blaring through D's stereo. Jade petty ass texted Kristy while we were on the way back and asked her to meet us at Ivan. So, guess who was waiting when we pulled up; everybody, including myself, burst out into laughter. We started drinking and continued to listen to music. I got out of the car and started twerking, I was two shots in, with a dab of lean. D got out of the car and got behind me. Kristy flared her eyes at me, and I kept dancing. *What was I supposed to do, stop having fun?*

People started to pull up and joined us. Before we knew it turned into a parking lot kickback. It was a vibe. The gathering moved from the parking lot to the stairs in front of Ivan. Jade took two or three shots of Cîroc the rest of the night she was drinking Corey's drink. I finished the bottle and started running my mouth. I walked over to almost every person outside and asked if they knew where Tali was. I almost walked to the girl in his dorms who he'd been fucking almost every night until D intersected. Fucking, Bro Code. Her name is Zara, she's from Cali, B. Simone thick and I hated her. She was fucking my man. She frowned her face up at me and then started to chuckle with her friend standing next to her. That would have made me feel like shit if I wasn't drunk. Zara gave Emmanuel and D a hug then walked in.

Tali's football friend Josh walked out, passing them. I don't know what she said to him, but I heard him say, "I really hate that bitch."

"Me too," I slurred

He was drunk af sipping on a drink he mixed in a Gatorade bottle. Josh was a typical light skin cutie. Most girls I know would have considered him to be more attractive than Tali, but with Tali, it was more than his looks. He had a swag to him, that hood twang. I walked up to him and asked him for a sip of his drink. I took about five sips, and no, I do not know where his mouth has been. Twenty-four year old me would NEVER. I was beyond drunk; I had mixed dark and light. I kept drinking to the point the liquor no longer was nasty. I don't know what triggered this to happen, but I ended up rolling around in the grass, talking about, "I want Tali. I want to fuck Tali. Tali. Tali come out here. I want Tali." Everyone outside was silent then burst into laughter. Tali came out, and I remember him walking away like he was embarrassed by me.

D got me up, and I threw up in the grass, getting some of it on my sock. I pulled it off and threw it. Jade was just as drunk as I was; she kept saying, "Who laughed at my bitch? Who tryna get hit? Bring Tali here. I'm gonna whoop his ass."

D and Emmanuel carried Jade and me back to Oliva Davidson, an all-girls dorm where Jade stayed. They got us to the elevator, Emmanuel left, but D stayed to make sure we got to her room. The elevator doors opened, and two girls with White Castle bags in their hand stared at us. They looked like they had just got caught fucking or something. One of the girls eventually smiled, and we walked in. D walked us to Jade's door, grabbed her key, and swiped us in. I opened up the door and jumped in the bed I claimed as my own. Jade was never assigned a roommate, so she made up the second bed like a guest bed. I got up to grab a plastic bag to hold next to me in case I threw up again. I dove back in bed and was sound asleep. I woke up so confused and hungover. Jade quickly got up, screaming, "We gotta get to the café to get breakfast before it closes," it was like she was dreaming breakfast food.

The café had set hours during the week. Monday through Friday, the café was open from 6 am- 10 am, 11 am – 3 pm for lunch, and 4:30 pm-7 pm for dinner. During the weekend, they were open from 8 am-noon for breakfast and 4 pm-7 pm for dinner. The three restaurants on campus hours weren't any better.

I told Jade I would meet her in the café after I showered. You know, back at my bougie dorms. I stayed in Patty

Hall, where the scholars and upperclassmen lived. It was easy for me to get in there despite all the people who said I wouldn't get in. I just applied for it, and since I went to a private high school, my GPA was bomb. Well, bomb enough to reach the dorm requirements.

A few days had passed, and the weekend approached. It was time for me to face Paul. I still couldn't get over Tali, and there was no longer a spark with Paul. Jade's brother came up to the school to take Jade home for the weekend, and I hitched a ride. My mom had already threatened me about adding unnecessary mileage to my car, so this was the best option. Paul met me at Jade's house and took me home. I was happy to see him until he opened his mouth. He always spoke about bullshit. Like nigha, where is your ambition? He wanted to tell me about a lick he hit. He noticed I was uninterested in his illegal shit, so he shifted the conversation towards me. He told me how proud he was of me, and that be bragged on me to his friends and family. He promised me he was working towards getting his GED, so he can go to college. I smiled and grabbed his hand, locking his fingers between mine.

We pulled up to my mom's, he parked his car in the dark cul-de-sac and kissed me. Paul's kisses were always soft and sweet. We continued to kiss and ended up in the back seat. He pulled my dress up and slid his man's inside. I wasn't wearing any panties, so he didn't have to pull 'em to the side. This sex felt good because I felt the passion, our "love," let my mom tell it, our "infatuation" for each other. He fucked me for a long five minutes (*rolls eyes*). He knew from our past experiences together; I did not fuck with quickies; the shit was wack. He immediately went down to apologize to

Lady with his tongue, trying to replace his dick. The main reason I disliked head is that it was too freaking sloppy. My box already wet, but this mutha fucka made a puddle, and it was his slob. I chalked it up as a lost and ended our night.

The weekend past and my vagina felt a little off. I was discharging, and I had a slight smell. To be honest, it was feeling a little off since the night I smashed Tali, but I thought it was my guilt. I have always been the paranoid type, maybe because, with Paul, I constantly got bacterial vaginosis (BV), which I blamed on the condoms we barely used, but I am now sure it was because he was friendly with his dick.

Bacterial vaginosis is a condition caused by the change in amount of bacteria in your vagina. Office of Women's Health states, BV occurs when you have more harmful bacteria than good. Similar to a yeast infection, you can get BV without having sex, but it is more common in women who are sexually active.

African American women are twice as likely to get BV than a white woman. Having sex with a new sex partner or more than one partner without condoms can increase your chances of this infection. -According to Healthline, women are more likely to develop symptoms when having sex with other women; however, men can carry this infection on their penis and possibly pass it from woman to woman without knowing.

He was my first. I LOVED him. *(*rolls eyes)*. I went to the city's local clinic. A fifth-year senior told me on the first day of classes that I shouldn't go to our school's clinic because if you had something, the doctor reported it and something about being a statistic in our school's database. *I'll pass.* If I'm going to be a statistic, I'd rather be one with the city, more people to compare.

I went, and she ran a culture. Shout out to this clinic because I didn't have to pay a dime. However, I did have to wait a good hour before being seen. I waited another hour for the doctor to come in and give me my culture exam. My legs were prompt up and spread wide. I got over being embarrassed by my over moist pussy, so I took a deep breath, and she stuck the surgical dildo up my vagina. It was so cold. She cranked it open, and it was uncomfortable. I felt like I instantly had cramps. She turned on the light, and once she looked under the scope, she was positive that I had Chlamydia.

Chlamydia is a sexual transmitted disease. It can affect both men and women, but it is most common in young women, according to Medline Plus. This disease can be passed even if you aren't experiencing symptoms which can include genital pain or discharge from the vagina or penis.

I remember her words exactly after she informed me of the diagnosis.

"Erica, you are a beautiful young lady. I'm telling you now more men than a little bit come in here daily for this and other diseases. You have to be careful and use preventative methods."

I was devastated. I didn't know who to blame. So, I attacked who I was comfortable with, Paul. I found out he cheated on me again. With his fat ass ex, Tiff. She was FUBU – "fat, ugly, black, and uncomfortable." Thank you, Tyler Perry. He went on and confessed, claiming he wore protection. Later on, he told me they fucked in the shower.

Stupid mf, do I look dumb?

I'm young, and sometimes I try to act like I don't see the facts, but this was very clear to me. I'm like ain't no way you wore a condom fucking her in the shower. Boy, bye. And that's the end of Paul's chapter.

I honestly wasn't sure if it was Paul or Tali who gave me this STD. I blamed Paul, but as I said, Lady felt weird as soon as Tali put his dick inside. I wrote it off, and I could never mention it to Tali. Why, you ask? I didn't want him to judge me or to try and flip it on me, like I gave it to him. Men do that, make you feel guilty for some shit you didn't even do.

Some time had passed, and I still hung out at Ivan Hall; I fell back from Tali. Well, I did until he seduced me Alpha party at Emma's. Kristy, Jade, and I got all dressed in our booty shorts and heels, well gym shoe's in Jade's case. Her tall ass was just as tall as me in my six-inch heels. Emma's didn't have the two for five dollars special, but we still got shots at the door. The Greeks were strolling all through the party. Everybody was there, having a good time. I saw James in the crowd; he looked so happy to see me. James came through the crowd and gave me a long, tight hug. I heard Kristy smack her lips, but I ignored it. He bought a round of shots and gave them to us. "Turn up," he said, then took his shot.

He gave me a peck on my cheek. I walked through the party stopping at every other song to twerk. Finally, we made it to the front near the DJ. The DJ started his eight minutes twerk mix with Do My Dance by Tyga and 2 Chainz, and I had to fuck it up. I slightly bent over, then put my hands on my knees and started to shake and pop my ass. The DJ kept playing hit after hit, and I heard what seemed to be people from Chicago's anthem, Bounce, and Break Yo Back. Next to me stood Zara dancing her ass off, better than the Chicago girls. She was swinging her arms and popping her ass simultaneously. Her ass was just bouncing. I learned the dance by watching her and added my own twang to it by getting down lower and staying there longer. My girls were hyping me up. The song ended, and I headed toward the bar for another drink. The DJ turned on my freshman year anthem Do It by Mykko Montana. Tali walked towards me, beefing it up, then turned me around. "You rubbing through my head while I'm in between yo legs," Tali screamed, repeating the lyrics of the song then bent me over.

I whined my hips against his groin. I wanted to remind him what he was missing out on; I just had to wait for the right moment.

The next night I was chillin' with my friends, we had a recap of the party, and I creamed my panties from the thought of fucking him again. This time I would be single, not that it mattered. I texted him, "I wanna fuck."

He responded, "*wya?*"

"In your dorm, in D room," I replied. See, D and I became great friends. He lowkey was the spy even though I now know he was feeding me bullshit.

He texted back, "Come out in the hall."

There he was along with five other guys just chilling in the crazy house looking hallway. I walked over toward him, and he opened his room door, let me in, and closed it behind him. He put on some Boosie and turned it all the way up. I felt the bass on my feet through the floor. He walked over to me. I stood there, staring at him. I leaned in for a kiss, but he turned me around. *WTF? Something wrong with my lips?* He bent me over, pulled my sweats down, and gave me five solid pumps before he stopped. I assumed he came. He walked over to his phone and turned on, "I was getting some head," by Shawnna, and raised the volume. I turned around to see if we were finished, and he said, "Give me some head." Now what you ain't gonna do is demand head like that. I don't suck everybody dick, and it's a turn off when I'm asked to do it by someone who ain't my man. I laughed at him to disguise my embarrassment and said, "You first."

"Nah," Tali responded. My heart raced as I pulled up my sweatpants. I felt like dog shit, but that wasn't even the icing on the cake. He pulled up his boxers and left his basketball shorts at his ankles and opened the door, still with the same song blasting.

I walked out and had to face the same five boys in the hall. They were the red shirt gang, also known as the benchwarmers on our football team. D and Jade were down the hall, pretending they didn't see what just happened. I was so embarrassed. That was the nail in the coffin. I was done, and to top it with a cherry, I later found out I had gotten HPV. At this time, I was unfamiliar with the facts of human papillomavirus (HPV). I had already gotten the Gardasil shots in high school; I thought it was to prevent it. Those three shots hurt like hell.

HPV is a common sexually transmitted infection. 79 million Americans are infected with HPV and most of them are in their late teens early twenties, according to The Centers for Disease Control and Prevention (CDC). This infection doesn't always show symptoms; however, it can still be passed during sex. **The Gardasil Shot** is a set of vaccines that prevents certain types of HPV. I received my first Gardasil vaccine in 2010, because my mother was familiar with HPV. She knew this vaccine would help protect against the greatest risk of the infection, cervical cancer.

I didn't know this information, so I didn't take it that seriously. I just knew it was something that could possibly go away in time, and it could lead to me not having children. I was conflicted, I wasn't sure if the doctor was wrong because I got the shots or if this was something that could really change my life. Tali was now dead to me, and I vowed that I would never be disrespected like that again, and never would I fuck him ever again. I still say to this day I fucked him one and a half times because them five shitty pumps count as a half since I ain't get my nut.

Chapter 7

Real Friends

A little later in the semester, I received a message from James. He asked what I was doing. I replied, "nothing and that I was in my dorm watching TV. "

See, I took a few weeks off from visiting Ivan Hall. I needed to move on. First, I couldn't stop hating Tali, but at the same time, I didn't want any bad blood between us. For some reason, I always gotta make sure we okay—*we*, as in any guy, I didn't want bad blood. Anyways, James responded and asked me if I wanted to come over and kick it with him. Lucky for me, my roommate finally decided to show her face that week. She suggested I go over to his house. "Talk to guys who live off-campus. You could do more," she said.

I'm not going to lie; I would have loved to fuck Thor, but my heart wasn't in it. I went over, and he answered the door shirtless. My eyes widen. *Oh my, oh my. Erica snap out of it.*

Lady commanded, "Abort, abort now. I will make you want to fuck him."

I walked into his townhome, and he guided me upstairs to his room. He had an actual bedroom set—a king-size oh-so-comfortable bed, full-size mirror, big enough to see two full bodies, and a couple of posters of himself.

I sat down on his bed, and he turned off the lights then joined me. He handed me the remote and told me to pick a movie. I turned it on Illegal Tender, kicked off my shoes, and slid up to the top of the bed with him. James took off his shorts and laid on his stomach, wearing nothing but black briefs.

"Come give me a massage," he said. "I'm sore from practice."

My eyes widened, and my heart raced as I imagined placing my hands on every inch of that muscled body. Did I mention James was the captain and QB for my school's football team? I couldn't believe I was in this situation. How lucky could I be? I swallowed thickly, nodded, and grabbed the baby oil off his dresser next to the TV.

I straddled his back and instantly felt Lady pulsate. I never really gave a full body massage before. I did see a few rub-down scenes in porn and movies, but it always led to sex. His back was smooth and firm, and his butt was tight and unnoticeable. Thank God because I prefer guys without big butts. His legs were ripped, and his calves sculpted. He was built like Thor. I admired the view. He shone so much; the TV lights reflected off his skin. After what seemed like an eternity of feeling him up, I told him I was finished, and he turned around and told me to massage the front of his body.

Tenting the sexy black briefs he wore, his dick stood at attention, waiting for me to ease its tension. I sat on top of his snake with nothing but his briefs and my thin ass panty-less leggings between us. I grabbed the oil and slowly drizzled it on James' chest. He flexed, making his chest jump and my pussy quiver. I rubbed his chest in circular motions, applying pressure with my thumb. Once I made it up to his neck, I don't know what came over me; I decided to massage his neck with my lips, giving him soft sweet kisses. I did the same to the other side, then James squeezed my ass and sat us up. He kissed me, bit my bottom lip, moved down to nibble on my ear, then he sucked on my neck, stoking a feeling I never experienced before. Was this how it felt to be with a grown-ass man? James was twenty-four at the time. We stopped kissing as soon as shit got real on the TV, and we cuddled until it was over. I had so much fun, and he didn't even pressure me to fuck. I honestly still felt like a virgin, like I needed some sort of permission to have sex like sex was wrong. I don't know, but I needed a break from sex, so I was happy James didn't pressure me because I know for a fact I would have given in.

I soon found out that Jade and Kristy had a class with James. He was the jock who used the smart gullible girl to help him with his work. Kristy talked about how she liked James and how she just wanted a chance with him for days. I chose not to tell Kristy about James and me, but Jade knew. We were leaving the café one day, and all Kristy talked about was how cute James was and how he followed her on Instagram. I followed them to Olivia Davidson (OD) to Kristy's room; she lived a few doors down from Jade. Kristy kept going on and on about James, all I could do was giggle. She went to the bathroom, and Jade grabbed her phone. We slid into James DM for her. We started the conversation like, "I know you have a game coming up the night before our project is due, you want me to help you?"

Kristy walked out of the bathroom and started to straighten up her room. Jade attempted to hide the phone behind her back, but the damn thing chimed then vibrated loudly. Kristy turned and saw me giggle then asked what we were doing with her phone. Jade ignored her question and checked the notification. It was a message from James, "Bet, you tryna come through tonight I live in Toucan Crest Apartments on the west side."

"Kristy, you got a date with James tonight," I yelled.

She leaned over the phone to see what I was talking about, and she saw James in her DMs. We deleted the first message, so she just saw him ask if she wanted to come over. She instantly ran back into her bathroom room and took a shower. Kristy lived in one of the suites at OD, so she only had to share a bathroom with her suitemates, like the rooms in my dorm. OD only had a few suites, so Kristy lucked up; Jade, not so much. She had to share showers with the rest of the floor.

Long story short, she went over to James' place, and he only wanted her to do his work. James wrapped up their evening right after she finished the project. I know because he was getting her out of there so I could come over. Shady shit, right? Well, not really. I found out Jade told Kristy about James and me. Jade told me right after Kristy left. Kristy chose not to care, so may the best girl win!

At that point, I wanted to be petty and really get under her skin. I arrived at James' house and parked a couple of cars down from where she parked. I had to make sure she saw me walk in before she pulled off. I knew she wasn't going to say anything; she wasn't a confrontational person.

The next day, our school had Midnight Madness. It's when the café opened up at night from 11 pm – 3 am, to serve chicken and waffles. One of the campus DJs came out and hosted the event. You could only come in if you had a ticket, and the only way to get a ticket was to use swipes or to attend our university's Town Hall meeting. Most students ran out of swipes within the first month of the semester buying snacks and fast food from the restaurants. The student government association (SGA) knew what they were doing; the town hall meeting was packed. The students had to stay until the end of the meeting before they could get a ticket. Jade and I had a few more swipes left, so we didn't go to the meeting. Kristy called herself being upset with me for talking to James and being upset at me meant not talking to Jade. She went off with some guys from the band down to Old Patty Hall, the freshmen dorm—the dorm that stayed lit but also stayed on lockdown. She missed Midnight Madness.

The DJ had the crowd swag surfin', and he shouted out my city. He played Mr. Miyagi, a Cincinnati song. I had the time of my life. The DJ changed the vibe by playing trap music, and chairs started to fly across the café. The party ended, and I didn't even get seconds. Everyone walked to the yard, and we ran into Kristy shit-faced drunk, screaming, "Erica fucked James; I can't believe Erica fucked JAMES."

I didn't, though.

Meeting in his bedroom

On February 8, I received my first arranged sex partner. I know this date because it was Jade's birthday and she told me that she found the perfect sex mate for me. I had been complaining about how I just wanted a guy to fuck me good and consistent. Jade started talking, and by talking, I mean fucking this guy Will, in her Robotics class. I'm not sure why she took Robotics when she studied prelaw. Will had a half-brother named JR, and they were roommates. In between one of Jade and Will's smash sessions, Jade and JR started talking about JR's sex life, and Jade told him she had the perfect girl for his needs.

What Jade didn't mention to me, was she already gave this guy the 4-1-1 on me. After she mentioned that she had found me a sex partner, she showed me his Instagram page, and I was impressed. He was a caramel delight with a little peach fuzz and somewhere between a bird chest and buff chest. Let's just say he was working on his abs.

A few days later, I was working, checking out this long line of students. You know the ones who waited to the last absolute moment to buy their books or the ones who tried to return their Beat headphones and Bluetooth speakers because they used up their book voucher buying everything but books, I saw JR in my line. I acted like I didn't notice him.

"So, you're E, Jade's friend," he said as he walked up to the front of my register, "she said you wanted a special friend." I couldn't help myself; I blushed. I was a little embarrassed. I didn't even know she told him about her plan.

"Yeah, I am," I said to my surprise. "I heard you the guy for the job."

He slid me his phone, and I put my number in. I was interrupted by my manager Mrs. Wyatt. She was in her mid-forties, and she reminded me of Dolly Parton. She walked up behind me.

"I'm not paying you to flirt with pretty boy over here," she said in her southern accent, casting him an appreciative glance. "I know I said to please the customers, but you don't have to PLEASE the customers."

JR almost died laughing. I was more shocked that he just came up to me so boldly like *you want this dick? Well, you better take this dick.* LOL. Don't mind me, but he was really BOLD.

My boldness quickly disappeared because the next time I saw him, he was in the staircase in Mayweather - the Education, Public Admin, Foreign Language, English, and Communication building. It also had a Starbucks inside with a mini-store. JR was with Will and Jade on the stairs. I felt ambushed, except I ran into them. Jade tried to make small talk, but I was more concerned about leaving all of them. I hurried and lunged up the stairs, skipping a couple at a time, and Miss G String pops up. Jade couldn't let it go, but before she could say anything, JR yelled, "I will be taking those off tonight. Thank you for the sneak peek."

I was so embarrassed.

Here I was trying not to be seen and end up being seen. I gotta big bark, small bite. *Well, at that moment, I did. My bite eventually got bigger.*

JR and I made some arrangements to hang out. The first day, we hung out with Will and Jade, but the next time we were in his room alone. For the record, I was still new to sex, so I high key got nervous, not knowing what I got myself into. I mean, it was ten at night. Why else would I be in his dorm that late? I knocked on his door, and a random guy answered. My heart dropped,

Inner voice: Bitch, how you gonna be an invisible thot, knocking on the wrong doors and shit?

I stood there, froze for a second. I froze because I quickly had to assess the situation; I looked at my phone, where JR's message thread appeared bright as day room 309. Random Guy looked at my confusion, turned around, and saw JR coming toward the door.

Inner voice: I know this is not Will because I know Will. So, who tf is that dude? Is this not a dick appointment? Why we got company?

JR guided me in then I noticed it was two dorm rooms in one. The two rooms shared the common area, which was basically the front door and restroom. I turned right toward JR's room, and he lowkey had the room sex ready. He dimmed the lights by turning off the room's main light and turned on the reading light on top of his headboard. He had some soft music playing, and we started playing Strip Speed, a card game he made up. The loser of each game had to take off a piece of clothing. I won, of course, because I'm a beast, so I started to talk my shit. JR leaned in to kiss me and then licked on my neck. I forgot all about my victory. JR's lips were so juicy. He got those bounce back lips; you know the ones where you push them in, and they bounce right back, like a trampoline. As he kissed my neck, he unclamped my bra then slid off my leggings. I lost two games, so I had to strip out of my t-shirt and one sock. He kissed my breasts, licking around my nipples, making them harden. He then slid his tongue down past my belly button.

Inner Voice: now, bitch, you know you don't even like head. Well, maybe you might like it this time.

I struggled a little as I tried using the bed to get my other sock off. I pressed my foot against the bed and slid it off. I took a deep breath as JR licked on my thighs. He spread my legs and lifted them up, making one big ole slippery mess. I grabbed his head, brought him back up, and said, "Fuck me."

Okay, counselor. I have to take a moment to breathe. I'm having flashbacks. Reliving my sex life with you is getting me a little hot.

Okay. JR must've liked what he heard because he bent down, started kissing me, rolled us over, pulling me on top of him, still sucking on my bottom lip. Pete was standing at attention. Yes, I named this man's penis on the spot. LOL. That thing was massive. He was his own person. My mouth watered, I just had to try it. I hadn't sucked dick since Paul, and since he was my first, I wasn't quite sure if I was terrific. But shit, I got the job done. I put my warm wet mouth over his shaft and did what I'd seen the white girls do in the pornos.

For some reason, I love playing with the tip, and when I hit his balls, I saw his legs bend, and his toes curl. This was the first time I had a guy call out my name. Now I have to be honest with you; he had some small balls but a huge dick. He was my first big dick. If compared to a Direct TV remote, Pete and the remote would tie. I'm not talking about the new remote, either. Ever since we fucked, I started to like a little pain. I want to feel Lady throb afterward.

To be honest, he was a false advertisement for men because I only ran into two more guys with huge dicks like him. I assumed older men would have bigger dicks. JR grabbed the condom and eased into me. He connected with my body, and I loved it. JR was a great fuck. I was no longer a grump, and I never went crazy on him; well except this one time.

JR would come over to my dorm periodically. We'd just hang out and watch a couple of movies, and then he'd bounce, or so I thought. My neighbor Jazz worked as a resident aid, and she saw he signed out when I walked him outside, and then, when I went back up to my room, this fucker signed right back in to see, guess who? HIS GIRLFRIEND. How the fuck did I not know he had a girlfriend. Let him tell it; they weren't together but were ready to try again. Well, what could I do but be pissed and complain to Jade about how she wasted my time? She was done with Will, just as fast as I was with JR.

Now that my head was out of Tali and JR's ass, I could finally breathe and be myself again. I spent more time in my dorm and working. I noticed a handsome, light-bright, young man named Harlem—a sophomore. We met one night on the elevators in our building. It was such an intense moment because I've never seen someone so damn handsome in person. He looked like he was coming back from a party, and I just got back from a snack run. If you watch Grey's Anatomy, you know all the ardent scenes happen in the elevator. I felt like Bow Wow and Ciara in the 'Like You' video. He got on the elevator first and held the door open for me. I thanked him, not noticing him. He asked me what floor I stayed on and our eyes locked. I didn't look a complete mess. I had my hair blown out in a ponytail, and I wore a pink JHU hoodie with black leggings. He gave me that look of certainty like he had to have me. Shit, I had to have him,

If you let my hating ass neighbor tell it, he wouldn't give me a second look; he's an asshole, and she tried to talk to him their freshmen year. He didn't give her a chance. I didn't believe her, though, because the way our eyes caught each other, he was interested. Harlem played his game real smooth. He found excuses to talk to me. One day, he randomly came up to me in the café wearing basketball shorts and a t-shirt with the sleeves cut off, showing off his sexy yellow body with all those tats on his arm.

"Erica, y'all sell mechanical pencils at the bookstore?" he asked. "How much they cost?"

"Yeah, silly," I responded. "It's a bookstore, but I have some in my room. I'll be back over there once I leave here, room 412."

I was shocked. I handled it so smoothly. I think the fact I wasn't on Harlem's ass made him desire me. He could have had any girl he wanted. I walked to my room and started to watch TV, and I heard a knock at my door.

Inner Voice: Harlem is on the other side of my door. OMG, OMG.

I jumped down from my tall ass bed and looked in the mirror to make sure I wasn't a hot mess. I grabbed the box of pencils and went to open the door. I tried to hand him the box, but instead, he walked in, grabbed the box, and tossed it on my dresser. He asked me what I was doing, then told me to put my number in his phone.

I entered my number and saved it as E. I handed him his phone, then he sat down and finished my TV show with me. I just knew he was going to be my bae.

*Twenty-four-year-old me: There yo ass go, walking
before you crawl. Why couldn't you have in your
mind he was going to be your friend...period?*

I walked Harlem out of my room, and my nosey ass neighbor saw him leaving. She ran into my room after he had left, screaming, "Girl. I can't believe Harlem was in your room."

I smiled and looked at my dresser, noticing the missing pencils. I guess he wanted them after all. I completely ignored her and focused on why this fine ass boy would want me. I know I'm beautiful. At least that's what people say, but I didn't feel beautiful. I got put down so much in middle school, I carried it with me, knowing I was above average but not drop-dead gorgeous. Harlem looked like he only cuffed light skin, no darker than light caramel girls with some pretty ass curly mixed girl hair, which classified her as DDG (drop-dead gorgeous. Keep up). Yes, I stereotyped him, but I based it on my experience. The light skin boys weren't checking for me in school; they were checking for the DDG type. No shade toward beautiful women who are lighter than I am; beauty is in the eye of the beholder, but let's face it, the eyes that typically looked at me did not find any beauty in chocolate. I guess college was different.

A few days after giving him my number, we started hanging out. It was weird, though; we hung out at night in his dorm room, and we never had sex. One night I came over, and his roommate was gone. Harlem and I laid in the bed and watched the Little Rascals. Well, I watched the Little Rascals. Harlem was knocked out as soon as we got under the covers on his XL Twin size bed. Midway through the movie, Harlem's roommate, Pretty Eyes (PE), came in. PE was so damn sexy, and I don't think he knew I was in the room because he started to strip.

Quick Question: Does that make me a perv when
I stared at him without him knowing?

PE took off his shirt. To this day, his back is imprinted in my brain. I was just eighteen looking at what I would call a grown-ass man back. PE is a dirty caramel with rugged hair, green eyes, and juicy lips. He started to take off his pants, and I heard him sing as his briefs fell to the floor. Even his ass was fit. Well, I guess it should be, considering he was the star of the track team. He free balled to the shower, and I could finally catch my breath. Now I saw it as I had two options: get my things, wake Harlem and tell him I was leaving or finish the movie, and then wake Harlem to go. I did neither.

I remained watching the movie, and PE came out of the shower, all wet, leaving the bathroom steamy. He had a towel draped around his sculpted waist, and he caught me staring. I was stuck looking at that athletic body and wondering what he was carrying under that towel. He dropped his towel and grabbed a fresh pair of briefs. After he slid them on, he gave me a wink and jumped into his bed. I turned over to Harlem; he finally woke up, turned off the TV, pulled me closer, and we went to sleep. I stayed until Harlem's morning practice alarm went off, then I went back up to my room.

Chapter 9

First Probate Spring 13

Harlem stopped hitting me up as much, and I couldn't stop wondering if PE told him I had been a peeping tom. I tried not to dwell on it too long because I stopped seeing him around campus. I found out he was on-line to be a nasty, nasty dog. I didn't know how I felt about that because the semester prior, a Que practically fucked me at a party with my damn clothes on. I mean, he picked me up, slid under me, and acted like he was eating my pussy through my pants. I was new to this HBCU lifestyle; they were wild. Besides that small hiccup, the dogs were pretty cool.

All Greeks have probates or a coming out.

The afternoon before the probate, Jade and I met up at Ivan Hall to pregame with a couple of guys who lived in Old Patty Hall—Kol and Kyrin. They both were from Cleveland, like Tali. I'm not sure if they all knew each other before college or not. I knew Kyrin from my freshman orientation class, and Kol was in my psychology class with this girl Dawn, my study buddy. I had a small beef with Kol because one day in class, I wore Jordan's, and he took a picture then posted it on Instagram, with the caption 'what are those?' I'll tell you what they were; they were my friends' shoes. She didn't want them anymore, so I took them. I shortly learned that Jordan's have "expiration dates." I have never been a shoe head, and I rarely wear gym shoes, so no, I didn't keep up with which Jordan's were the right ones to get. I got over that beef, but of course, I brought it up when we got to the room.

Kol poured me a shot of E&J and told me to simmer down. Jade and Kol had this flirting thing going on, and Kyrin tried it with me, but I boxed his ass out. *No shot here.* I saw Dawn in the hallway and followed her to her room so I could finish getting drunk, and then it happened. I popped my bubble. I was fucked up once again; this time, I didn't throw up. We all walked outside, excited to see our first probate. It was right outside of Ivan hall, directly in front of the library. It was thick af. Everybody pushed and shoved, and the Ques hadn't even walked down yet. Once the Ques made their way across the yard to the front of the library, our front-row seat, we worked so hard to get became a nosebleed seat real fast. All I kept hearing was "step back, step back," and I heard myself screaming, "Harlem, I want to see Harlem. I love you, Harlem. I am fucking a dog tonight." My thirsty ass.

The show started, and I couldn't see over the large crowd of people. So, I decided to stand on a random ass wooden chair someone must've taken from the dorms to get a better view. Not so sure that was a good idea.

When the show ended, everybody started to head to a new club, Blackout, for the afterparty. I knew we were too drunk to drive ourselves, so I grabbed Dawn and Jade to find our new friend Tony. We met Tony at our school's Rec Center, Jade and I were coming up from checking out the pool. She wanted to get a basketball so she could shoot around, but she didn't have her student ID with her. She left her ID, in my car, parked at my dorm, way across campus. Tony was in charge of checking out gym equipment to the students, and Jade told him about all of her trials and tribulations to why she didn't have her ID. We all talked until the gym closed, she forgot all about the basketball.

I was the only one with a car, so I had to trust and pray Tony would drive my car like he would lose his life if something were to happen to it. I tried my hardest to sober up; I wanted to be as alert as possible. Tony assured me he was an excellent driver besides that time he wrecked him mom's car. My heart stopped; he burst into laughter and grabbed my keys. I said my silent prayer, and we made it. The party was literally down the street less than a mile away. Tony drove us down to the party. The bitch was lit. The DJ was jamming and brought out a big group from Chicago to turn up with us.

I was so gone I remember bits and pieces of the night. I remember getting on stage and twerking my ass off. Who brought me on stage, you ask? My damn self. I was turnt, and the DJ kept hyping me up. The artist smacked my ass, and the crowd threw money. I didn't get to see any of that money; Jade left the shit on the stage. I don't even think Harlem made it to the party.

The next morning, I felt paralyzed. My back was tighter than ever. I could barely move, and I didn't know why. I made it into work, and Mrs. Wyatt walked up and asked, "What your drunk ass do to yourself now?" She always was straight forward with me. She never sugar-coated anything, and for some reason, I was candid with her. I could not tell her what I had done this time, though, because I had no idea. I felt like I woke up that way. I wasn't left in suspense too long before Dawn walked into the store apologizing. I was baffled. I immediately asked her what I did last night because my back was on fire.

Dawn pulled out her phone and played a video. I interrupted her like, "Girl, I saw the probate."

Dawn said, "Shhh, just listen."

I turned up the volume, and all you hear is me yelling, "Dawn, help. Help. They're pushing me back. Dawn, help." I heard the sound of the chair I stood on pushed back. Then there was the sound of me tumbling down. My ass fell out of the chair and hit the concrete hard af, and then bounced back up like nothing had happened. Thank God I wasn't paralyzed.

Harlem completely stopped hitting me up at this point. Mind you; it had been three days since the probate. So, I was done crushing on him.

Later, Jade and I left the café and ran into Keith, the party promoter from Dayton, and he had the DJ with him. The DJ started talking to me, telling me how lit I was on the stage and asked me how much money I brought home. I gave Jade a hateful look because he was now the fifth person to ask me about the profits I never received. Jade was a horrible manager. We exchanged numbers, and Jade and I ended up at the village apartments across from the campus where the DJ lived with his roommate.

Their place was a total man cave—big paintings of naked black women all over the place and a wall full of signatures from the people who came to their spot. I signed my name somewhere; certain it would eventually get covered. Jade's ass wrote her name big as hell with a crown over the J. Mr. DJ poured us some drinks. All of the conversations got real juicy, really quick. It was like my first dose of being an adult because these men were like twenty-five at the time, and I was eighteen going on nineteen.

The main topic came up. The DJ said, "every girl likes head," and Jade agreed, but I quickly countered, "I don't like head, and I personally prefer dick over head."

"Well, you just haven't gotten it done right," the DJ replied.

He gave me that look, and I knew we were gonna fuck, but the shit got messier than that. I mean that literally and figuratively.

A couple of days passed, and the DJ and I were texting non-stop. *I'm just gonna call him DJ.* He invited me over to chill. I went over, and he opened the door, then led me to his room. I grabbed a couple of movies from the Redbox before I stopped by and somehow convinced him to watch The Life of Pi. That movie felt like it was on forever. It was so much more interesting the first time I watched it with my mom a few weeks prior. Needless to say, he fired my ass from picking movies. We joked around for a little bit, then I left and went back to my dorms.

A big party at the Warehouse Live was coming up, and my DJ was one of the DJs for the night. We only had a few club-like spots by my school. Most of the time, we had to travel. Warehouse Live was about thirty minutes from the school. My girls and I got all cute and popped up at the party. When DJ saw me, he instantly gave me a shout out through the mic. He stayed doing that shit. He came down and showed me so much, love. As soon as he got in arms' reach, he grabbed me and gave me the "boyfriend hug." I guess marking his future territory. He looked at me like he wanted to lift my pencil skirt and eat my pussy right there in front of everybody. The party went on, and my girls and I left.

So, Doc; I'm not sure why, when guys show me to much PDA, I fall back. It's like I don't want everybody knowing I'm fucking with you if we aren't official? I also don't like people in my business; I like to keep people wondering. So yeah, the hug made me slightly uncomfortable, but at the same time, I liked it. Out of all the girls there, he shouted me out, showed me, love.

I made it home, took a shower, and right when I was about to put on my nightclothes; I got a text from DJ telling me to stay the night with him. I threw on my big booty sweatpants and a beater with no bra. I grabbed my keys and was out. It's crazy; I didn't give it a second thought; I knew I wanted some dick, and I was still drunk, so sex was definitely in the air.

I knocked on the door, and he answered almost immediately. "Damn, E. You looked fine as hell tonight. Did you have fun?" he asked.

"Yea, I had a blast," I replied. We hugged and walked to his room.

I heard a goofy voice from the kitchen.

"Damn E, I ain't know you had an ass like that," DJ's roommate, T.Q., said.

I turned my head to him, but before I could respond, DJ's rachet ass said, "yeah, her ass been poking all night." We burst out laughing. Shit, I felt like it was the pants, but maybe I did have a fat ass. *Hype me up then.*

We walked inside his room, and I started to strip out of my clothes and jumped into bed, but before I could, he made to take a shot of Paul Mason. He had a grown-up room. He had a tall Queen-size bed with a red comforter. Now that I think about it, his room looked like a female was behind the design, but I didn't ask those questions. If you're pursuing me, especially in public, you must be single. DJ complimented my skin and leaned over to kiss my lips. His kiss was passionate like our lips matched. He continued to kiss me and moved down to my neck. OMG. I'm about to have real grown-up sex, I thought to myself.

DJ rubbed his tongue around my areola then gave it a light suck. Baby Boy was definitely about the four play. He went over to the other titty and did the same. This was the moment I realized I liked my titties sucked. DJ gave me soft kisses all the way down past my belly button, kissing my kitty cat before taking off my panties. The panties were barely off, and I felt her throbbing, ready for him. He went down to finish his meal, and he kept looking up at me in between each lick. This had me a little stuck because I could not figure out what to do with my hands, and I couldn't figure out if I was supposed to return the looks. The head wasn't horrible, but I still couldn't figure out why my homegirls preferred head over sex. Dick me down, PLEASE. She already wet; she doesn't need any help.

Relax. That Erica was young and inexperienced. I'm older now and have received A1 head. I definitely like and want it, but oral sex will never go before sex unless my partner is that wack, and if that's the case, why am I fucking him?

Okay, okay, back to it. Sorry, I get sidetracked; I'm trying to answer all of your questions! You keeping up?

Once he came up for air, DJ pulled off his shirt. He was the biggest guy I ever talked to. As soon as I started to get discouraged by his extended belly, I looked up at his pretty brown eyes and was ready again – "SHE READY" in my Tiffany Haddish voice. He leaned down to kiss me and got up to take off his sweats. You know what I was looking for.

Older me: Girl yo ass should have done the touch test a long time ago.

Did he pass? Yea, he did. I'm not sure if he would please me now, but I was in HEAVEN when I was eighteen.

He got on top of me, licked his two fingers, and rubbed them against my clit then spat on Lady.

For the life of me, I still don't understand why men do
that. She already wet. So, wtf is it for? I hate spit.

He stuck his thick chocolate delight inside. To be honest, I reacted like Monica from Love and Basketball, the same gasp and all. Once again, NO CONDOM. I don't know when kids are gonna learn. I took way too many uncalculated risks. Like I was Queen Invincible. He felt so good inside of me, though. DJ got up, pulled me to the edge of the bed, and flipped me over.

I thought I was about to get the ultimate back shots, but he bent down and started giving me head from the back. I felt like I was in a porn film. He grabbed me by my waist to pick me up, never missing a lick. He ate me out for a while, and in my head, I remember thinking damn this man is strong, please don't drop me on my head. After I got out of my thoughts, I realized his dick was out and, in my face, looking like the perfect thing to lick. I gave him head. I guess he wasn't ready; he had to take a seat on the bed. DJ laid back, and I un-straddled his face, thankful for the safe landing, and got on my knees to give him the thrill of his life. I licked the tip then put my mouth around the head. My favorite part is to smack the dick on my lips right before I put it back in my mouth, twirling my tongue around it. I got back up, and it was time to ride. We had a good three rounds that night. He always found his way up.

I wish I didn't take his gift for granted because older men aren't putting up fights. They get KO'd, thinking they put in some work.

We went to sleep, and the next morning, I was hit with another disappointment, stretch marks. We were lying in bed, and he sat up to get out of bed. Right on the side of his extended belly were stretchmarks. YUCK. That was a deal-breaker. I left his place, and I called Dawn soon as I pulled back into the dorms. "Bitch, he got stretch marks. I fucked a nigha with stretch marks."

I don't know why, but I felt like I wanted to share this awkward moment with Dawn instead of Jade.

Sad to say, that wasn't the last of DJ.

The semester went on, and I kicked it with his ass faithfully. He stayed giving me shout outs at the parties and coming in to flirt with me at the bookstore. The week before finals, I got a call from my dad at three in the morning, telling me my grandfather passed away and I was heartbroken. I couldn't make it to the funeral because I had to take my finals.

I walked around the entire campus, looking like a sad puppy. I walked through the yard where SGA was setting up for an event to end campaign week. DJ was setting up his equipment for the yard party, and he noticed I looked down. I couldn't even talk to him about it; I just told him I would text him, and I walked in the Student Center. I texted him a little later, and he made me stay at his place that night. He said he wanted to make sure I was okay.

Wasn't that a sign he cared? Wasn't that a sign he seen a future with me?

This is where I get confused in every situation-ship. I was lying in DJ's bed right after a good two rounds of bomb ass sex, looking at the ceiling, thinking about my granddad. This was my first lost, no one close to me had died before, and I couldn't figure out how to deal with it. So, I didn't. I shed a few tears dand tried to bury it. Another thing I couldn't stop thinking about was how my grandmother lost her love of fifty-five years.

How could I be with someone for so long just to lose them?

I took my finals. I'm not going to lie; I cheated my ass off on that SCI 102. Shit, our Turn Up or Transfer slogan almost screwed me. I quickly changed my motto to "it's better to cheat than repeat." That final was going to be fifty-one percent of my final grade. I typed up my cheat sheet, inserting every vocab word and formula. Then I made the words size 8-point Calibri font. I changed the margins so that all the words shifted to the left. Any terms that didn't fit, I moved to the next page and shifted them to the right. I bolded the words I needed to point out and printed double-sided. I cut it out and walked into class with my head held high.

I have never been the cheating type because I always get caught—not that day. I sat in my regular seat next to one of the class geeks, not your typical class geek, just a smart white girl. She fucked with me because I looked out for her once at the bookstore. I wore a skirt and put my cheat sheet underneath my thigh. Professor Nguyen was on it that day. It's like she got an inside tip that people were going to be cheating. She kept walking around in class. Her ass usually was the 'glued to her seat' type. I moved the paper from underneath my thigh and put it under my exam. I looked over at my neighbor's test for the rest of the answers. Not to toot my own horn, but ya girl did pass the class with an eighty-nine percent. I ended the semester on the dean's list.

DJ and I attempted to wrap things up because I had to go back home for the summer. It was time to move off of campus, and Lord knows I bought way too much stuff throughout the school year, so everything could not ride back with me in my little two-door Civic. DJ didn't have a car or time to help me move anything to the storage, so I went out on a limb. Well, not a limb in entirety.

Okay, you got me. I've been withholding some information. Before my granddad died, Tali and I started communicating again. Nothing much, I wasn't on his ass like I was first semester. He randomly texted me what's up one day, and we just started being friendly. One day, he was sick, and I wanted to be Captain Save-a-Hoe. I went to the grocery store and bought him a pack of Gatorade and some cough medicine along with some orange juice. I had to keep it "player." That was some shit Tali would always say. "Just keep it, player." I guess meaning STOP GEEKIN, be chill.

I brought him his stuff, and I went on my way. No pressure. I guess he liked that because he was back on the chase. But my head was wrapped up in DJ, and I know Tali was fucking all kinds of females. He had an entire team. Nothing more happened then. Time went by, and I didn't reach out to him again until I needed help moving my things into storage. I hit Tali up, and he came to the rescue. Tali pulled up and parked behind me, right outside the atrium of Patty Hall. He was so freaking manly. He didn't let me grab anything. He loaded up both of our cars and followed me to the storage unit. When I opened up the storage door, Tali was ready to unload. Afterward, I walked over to thank him, and the chemistry, the vibe, connection whatever you want to call it was overwhelming. He thanked me for getting him together while he was sick, and I thanked him for helping me out. He said, "E, I always got you."

Now somebody, please tell me what in the hell that was supposed to mean?

But did I ask questions? No. The shit sounded good and even made me a little moist. Was it because he made me feel wanted? Is that the pattern?

We were so close to kissing like those intense moments we see in the movies. I literally felt his breath on my lips, but I backed away, smiled, and thanked him again. He bit his bottom lip then turned to get in his car. That damn lip bite felt stamped in my mind.

Summer Break

I went on a two-week vacation with my dad and family. The entire two weeks, I could not get Tali or DJ out of my head, but Tali had to be shoved deep down. I promised myself I would never let a man play me the way he did, and I would never fuck him again. I texted DJ nonstop, sending thirst traps; he was my boyfriend. He just didn't know.

I made it back to Cincinnati and found my new bed, my momma's couch. I guess I should have never told my mom I couldn't wait to move out and go to college. She claimed she didn't know we had to come back, but I think she was just proving a point. In between sleeping on the couch and in my little sister's room, I just knew I had to move off-campus and get my own place. I was used to coming and going as I pleased, no one to question my every action. Not in my momma house. Where are you going? How long are you gonna be gone? You bet not wake me up coming in here all late or WE gonna have a BIG problem.

Blah blah blah.

I get it. Now that I am older and have my own place, I like things done a certain way, and if I have friends and family stay over, they bet not wake me up out of my sleep coming in. As a matter of fact, I would set the alarm before I go to sleep, so you better get in before I go to sleep or get yourself a hotel/Airbnb.

I saw a flyer on Instagram saying that DJ was hosting a mixer at a predominately white institution (PWI) across the river. I took my best friend Blake with me. She always went with the flow. We got a bottle, yes, we were under-age but come on now; she went to Eugene T. University in Alabama, and I went to Jackson H in Kentucky. Both schools were dead in the middle of the country. If not for anything, we found a way to get liquor. I pulled in the park-ing lot and parked. I didn't know that this party was on campus. Okay, yes, the word mixer on the flyer should have given me a clue, but it didn't.

My scary-ass was scared to pour-up on those grounds. We ain't know shit about the rules at a PWI. Fuck it; we poured up anyway. I hid the bottle in my trunk, and we walked in ten minutes later. The party was cool, but it wasn't a Jackson H party. It had good music until DJ had to be relieved. It had the people, a complete mixture of Black, white, and others standing around in groups or cliques. It didn't have our energy, our Greeks strolling and telling yo ass "to move" as they hopped, shimmied, threw up their pyramids, or even shook out their hair. Historical Black Universities have this vibe, and it just felt like I belonged.

What school did you graduate from? You did graduate,
right, or are you just giving me advice based on experiences?
You right, this is a free session. Let me just get this out.

DJ gave me a shout out as soon as we walked in. "Erica's fine ass just walked in the building," he shouted through the mic.

We couldn't get in the door good before Keith, the party promoter, was on Blake's ass. "E, who is this beautiful woman you've been hiding," Keith asked, grabbing Blake's hand to kiss it. His smooth-talking ass.

I'm going to tell you this right now if I know you ain't shit, I'm going to let my girls know. If my girl goes for you cool, at least she knows, and I expect the same from them. I told her straight up. "Girl, he lives with his baby mama in Richmond."

She laughed, and we went on about our business. DJ came down and met me in the crowd, I introduced him to Blake, and he gave me the most snuggly hug, grabbing my ass and peppering kisses on my lips. He gave Blake and me another shout out before we left and headed back home.

I dropped Blake off at home after we waited in White Castle's drive-thru for what felt like an hour. I made it to my house just before 4 a.m. I opened the door, and the screen slammed behind me. My momma is like a lion; she doesn't attack fast. She waits until you get good and comfortable before she dives in. In my case, it was a couple of weeks later. She acts more like a Gemini than me sometimes, and she's a Cancer.

She mentioned something to me about me, not respecting her house. She was upset because I didn't want to do the dishes which I did not use. Keep in mind, I had a younger sibling who lived there and used most of the dishes. She told me as long as I lived in her house, my sister will never have to touch a dish; I blew a gasket. I don't know why but that hit a nerve.

I walked out and got in my car. I just needed time. I went to the gas station to fill up my tank, and DJ sent me a text asking what I was doing.

I texted back, "On my way to come see you. My mom just pissed me off."

He texted back and said, "pull up."

He was preparing for an interview with this female entertainer from Chicago, his hometown. I pulled up to the Village apartments about two hours later, welcomed in with a bourbon shot. I couldn't even get comfortable. After I took the shot, DJ said, "You ready? We about to hit campus so I can use the studio to do this interview." I dropped my stuff off in his room, and he followed me in then closed the door.

He lifted my blue bodycon dress and smacked my ass. I got on top of the bed, arching my back to show off my pink-laced thong. He kissed my chocolate ass and made his way down. He was so freaky. I think I learned how to have real sex with him. He moved my thong to the side and stuck all 7.5 inches of himself inside me. His dick matched his size, so it was chunky, and it was everything to me at that moment.

We freshened up and went to campus to do his interview, which was a success. He was so excited. We went to Wendy's, and he asked me what I wanted. I was young and dumb then, I still kind of am, but anyway, I said, "nothing."

He told me straight up, "E, when a man asks you what you want, you better tell him."

I was taught to be independent, and I had cases where a guy thinks you owe him something because he got you something simple as a Wendy's four for four. Fuck outta here.

I took him up on his offer because I was hungry. We got back to his place and finished our food. Later we walked over to his homegirl Diamonte's place. She lived a few buildings up near the entrance of DJ's apartment complex. Canon, the SGA president, was over, and we were all drinking Carlos Russe wine and gossiping. I found out so much like the Provost was paying off two girls on campus to get abortions because he was fucking them while trying to get his wife, the Executive Associate Director of Communications pregnant. I found out the VP of Student Affairs had been sleeping over at the President's mansion. Look at me—a freshman. Well, I guess now a sophomore, getting all the tea from the SGA president and Diamante, Jackson H's walking gossip blog.

DJ and I had some real freaky sex that night. We never wore a condom, and he started finishing in me, ever since he found out I was on the shot. We got one more round in the morning before I headed back home. Confession: I smell everything, and I guess I had ADP, a term I learned from Tĕlo, a guy I met my sophomore year. It means 'all day pussy.' I grabbed my underwear and balled it up under the pillow so he wouldn't smell. I know that was nasty, but he never said anything. I went home on such a high. A couple of weeks passed, and Blake threw a back from school kick back in her mom's penthouse. Blake's mom was a flight attendant, so whenever she wasn't home, she was cool with Blake throwing little parties.

Right before the kickback, Legend, a guy I used to call my bestie in high school, hit me up. He noticed my body had started to fill out. My ass got fatter, and my breasts were sitting nice. He must have been checking out my Instagram. That was only the beginning of my thickness. He basically hit me up to ask if I was going to the kickback. Then he flat out asked if he could fuck me. I said, "Nah, that ain't gonna happen."

He was like we gone fuck tonight. I laughed it off. Everybody from our high school was at the party. There were a couple of people we knew from outside of the school, but it was a vibe. Liquor and weed everywhere. I threw back shots, and so did Legend. Justice came to sit next to me and whispered, "Bitch, I think they laced the weed with shrooms."

Thank God I didn't smoke because my scary ass would have panicked. I don't remember much about that night. I remember Legend and I kissing, and I was feeling his soft ass lips. I remember telling Justice, "Girl, I'm horny and drunk as hell. Please don't let me fuck Legend."

The next morning, I woke up and noticed my pussy was sore. When I went to the bathroom, I noticed a little blood. Last night's memories slowly returned when I flushed the toilet. I remembered being in the bathroom, bent over, fucking Legend over the tub. He was going in, and I guess I liked it. I remember pulling the condom off his dick. He hesitated at first, but he finished pounding my shit. I also remember Justice banging on the door like, "Are y'all fucking? Make sure you wear a condom," and slid one under the door.

FUCKING TEENAGERS RIGHT. Sorry, we were only nineteen.

When I left the bathroom, I was ready to go home. Guess who met me at the door, Legend. He was all happy go lucky as we walked down the hallway to the elevator. Once we got on, I flat out asked him, "Did you fuck me last night?"

Was I raped? I was disgusted with myself after that, and he and I were never the same. He kicked it with Justice one night, and she came to swoop me up. We all went to the waffle house, and Legend was on it. He texted me after we dropped him back off at home, begging me to come over so he could fuck one more time. I never spoke to him since.

Seriously, was I raped?

A little time passed, and it was Sunday—time for church. I pulled up all late and shit. I'd been coming late ever since I'd been back. I saw Dante in his mom's truck, kicking it. He told me to get in, and we found ourselves kissing and rubbing in her back seat. I told him to ride with me, and we went back to my mom's house. We went to my little sister's room and fucked on the bed. I swear Dante had a satisfying size penis. It was at least seven inches, and it was thick and chocolate, but he was always a waste of a fuck. He claimed to have a girlfriend back at school. Yes, my fast ass was being a side piece once again for this boy. His girlfriend must not have shown him how to fuck. After we finished like five minutes later, we got up and cleaned up. He asked me about school and who I fucked with. He was concerned like we were together. Shit like that confused me because I took that as he cared about me.

My PH balance was off, and I just had to make it to the doctor. I had discharge as usual, but I also was nervous because I just fucked three dudes within six weeks without condoms.

DUMB ASS.

The doctor checked, and after she heard the answers to the assessment, I felt like she was dead set on me having either Chlamydia or Trich. She gave me a prescription for four nasty, big ass pink pills, and fluconazole because antibiotics always give me a yeast infection. Doc told me she would call me within a week when my culture results came back. I was heated, and I don't know why, but I went straight after DJ. I asked him what bitches he been fucking because he gave me Chlamydia. I found out some truths that night. He told me-

Wait, my time is up? When is our next session? You didn't give me any feedback; you just been writing this entire time.

From the desk of: _______________________________

Client Name: *Erica Black*

Insane

Insane

Insane

Insane

Insane

Insane

Insane

9 781662 900433